Other Fred Carver Mysteries by
John Lutz
From Avon Books

FLAME
KISS
SCORCHER
TROPICAL HEAT

Bloodfire

A FRED CARVER MYSTERY

JOHN LUTZ

AVON BOOKS ◢ NEW YORK

AVON BOOKS
A division of
The Hearst Corporation
1350 Avenue of the Americas
New York, New York 10019

Copyright © 1991 by John Lutz
Published by arrangement with Henry Holt and Company, Inc.
Library of Congress Catalog Card Number: 90-32332
ISBN: 0-380-71446-9

First Avon Books Printing: January 1992

AVON TRADEMARK REG. U.S. PAT. OFF. AND IN OTHER COUNTRIES, MARCA REGISTRADA, HECHO EN U.S.A.

Printed in the U.S.A.

RA 10 9 8 7 6 5 4 3 2 1

For Ben

Thus at the flaming forge of life
Our fortunes must be wrought;
Thus on its sounding anvil shaped
Each burning deed and thought.
> —LONGFELLOW
> *The Village Blacksmith*

It is not in our power to love or hate,
For will in us is over-rul'd by fate.
> —MARLOWE
> *Hero and Leander*

Bloodfire

1

THE OCEAN roared and pushed him close to shore. Carver felt the equilibrium lent by deep water desert him. His toes and palms scraped on the grit and broken shells of sea-tossed sand. Breakers curled and flattened out, then frothed around his suddenly heavy and awkward body, which belonged to land. Dragging his bad leg, he crawled through shallow water toward the beach.

As he emerged from the water, the fierce Florida sun bore down on him. Almost immediately perspiration began to mix with seawater on his shoulders and the back of his neck. Carver wasn't afraid of sunburn; he was already brown from morning after morning of therapeutic swims in the sea.

He crawled to where his cane jutted from the sand like a spear. Picked up the folded towel next to it, shook sand into the burning morning air, and rubbed his face and bald pate with the rough terry cloth. Then he sat with his permanently stiff left leg extended, his good leg doubled under, and stared out to sea. In the distance a mammoth freighter lay on the hazy blue horizon like an island, its progress almost imperceptible as it made its way north. Closer in were several triangular white sails, banked at precisely the same sharp angle into the breeze. Above them half a dozen gulls, dark specks against a luminous perfect sky, dipped and soared on currents of warm air.

Carver loved to look out at the ocean, to sit and listen to the eons-old rhythmic roar of waves rolling in and crashing on soft sand, while he breathed in the fetid fish-rot scent of things living and dying and being cleansed by time and water. Between the smashing and sighing of surf, he could hear an occasional muted shriek; tanned sun worshipers were already on the public beach, to the right of where the shore curved away from his cottage with its private stretch of sand.

Only a small portion of the beach was visible. Carver saw a slender girl in a white one-piece suit dash into the surf and leap as if the sea were electrified. She screamed to someone onshore, then shook her long blond hair and ran back from the waves' reach and out of sight beyond the curve of land. Another scream. Laughter.

Movement caught his eye. A man was walking toward him from the direction of the public beach.

Carver bowed his head slightly and continued facing the ocean, as if he weren't watching the interloper. The man looked about average height and weight but was very muscular. He was suntanned evenly, as if he spent a lot of time outdoors, and was wearing red bikini trunks, stretched taut across a flat stomach. In his right hand was a wadded white towel. The heels of his rubber beach thongs flopped loosely and flicked up rooster tails of sand with each step.

Carver expected him to walk past, cutting through to the rocky beach on the left, which was too rough for swimming or sunbathing. He sat listening to the whisper of footfalls in sand as the man trudged behind him.

The swish of sand kicked up by the beach thongs stopped. The man was standing behind Carver.

Carver turned. The man was staring down at him. A guy about forty but still in great condition. The tan was almost too even, as if it had been augmented by sunlamps. He was handsome in a dark and classic way, though his wavy black hair was going gray. One of his thick, dark eyebrows was set higher than the other. Now it crawled even higher on his forehead, giving him a supercilious, amused look, as if he were passing through a world of inferiors he viewed with disdain. He had brown eyes, flashed perfect teeth as he smiled and said, "Enjoy your swim?"

"Always do," Carver said, making a point of staring out to sea, waiting for the man to resume walking.

Instead he moved around in front of Carver, facing the wide ocean. There was something haughty even in the way he stood.

Carver didn't feel like making small or large talk with anyone. "Private beach down here," he said, keeping his voice amiable. "I don't mind if you cut through, though."

"You're not very polite," the man said, not turning around. "Be that way, you'll scare off business."

"Business?"

Now he turned and did that amused, arrogant thing with his eyebrows: Carver was hardly worth his time, but here he was and Carver was a fool not to be glad. "You're a private investigator, right, Mr. Carver?"

"That's right. My office is in town, on Magellan Avenue across from city hall."

"That the only place you do business?"

"No," Carver said, deciding he was being a hard-ass when it wasn't necessary. Wasn't Edwina always warning him he was too cynical? That he was wearing out his life from the inside? He gripped his cane halfway up the shaft and used it to lever himself to his feet. He looked the man in the eye, smiled, and said, "You business?"

"I might turn out to be a client, if you want the case." He extended his right hand. "Name's Bob Ghostly."

Carver shook hands with the man, whose grip was powerful and dry an contained a hint of strength in reserve. "You know my name."

"Not your first."

"Fred, then," Carver said, thinking there was really no need for first names if this was business. "Usually I'm just called Carver."

"Okay, Carver." Again the affable handsome smile,

marred only by the disdainful eyebrows. "So you wanna hear my problem?"

"Let's go into my cottage," Carver said. "Cooler there. And I feel like drinking a beer."

"Sounds fine."

Carver tucked his folded towel under his arm and led the way up the gently sloping beach toward the low, clapboard cottage with its flat roof. He had to walk carefully with his cane in the soft sand, making sure its tip was planted firmly enough before leaning his weight on it. He could hear the slow, even tread of the man behind him, now and then the spray of sand and the slap of a rubber sole on a bare heel. Ghostly was hanging back, as if he didn't want to offend Carver with the fact that he had two strong and capable legs. Or maybe Carver was just reading it that way, filtering it through is own self-pity. Had to watch out for that.

He pulled open the screen door, then stepped aside on the plank porch so that Ghostly could enter first. Followed him inside and let the door slam shut behind him. The slap of wood against wood as it bounced several times off the doorjamb reverberated but was absorbed by the background sigh of the sea, lost in eternity.

Ghostly stood and looked around at the one-room cottage, the wood floor, the folding screen divider that sectioned off where Carver slept, the cooking area set off by a breakfast counter where Carver usually ate standing up, leaning as if he weren't lame. A row of dead plants, in pots dangling by chains, was silhouetted inside the wide window that looked out at the Atlantic. Ghostly said, "Nice place," as if he didn't mean it.

Carver tossed the damp towel in the canvas director's chair near the door. He thumped across the floor to the old refrigerator and opened the door. Cold air tumbled out on his bare feet. He reached in and closed his hand around an icy red-and-white can. "Want a Budweiser?" he asked. "That's all I got."

"You said it," Ghostly told him. "I don't see any sign of food in there."

Carver straightened up and stared at him. "You want the beer?"

"No, thanks." Ghostly was smiling, working those expressive out-of-sync eyebrows. Carver was beginning to think the guy was a smartass trying to be sociable and not quite making it. A nasty edge kept showing through.

Carver tugged at the can's pull-tab, heard the hiss, and felt cold liquid dribble on the webbing between his thumb and forefinger. He took a long pull on the beer, not minding that it stung his throat a little going down, then backhanded foam from his upper lip. "So what's your problem, Mr. Ghostly?"

"My wife."

Now Carver had to tame a smile. The old story. That was what kept him in business, trouble between the sexes. Love, lust, whatever, really did make the world go round, dropping people off at Carver's door.

He clutched the crook of his cane in one hand, the beer can in the other, and limped over to the director's chair, still trailing water on the floor. He used the cane to lower himself into the chair, on top of the towel. He always sat in this chair when he was finished swimming, and didn't mind if the canvas seat and back got wet. He took another swallow of beer and waited for Ghostly to continue.

"She's missing," Ghostly said.

Carver thought, How original. Said nothing.

Ghostly gnawed his lower lip, letting Carver know how concerned he was. "Last week I woke up and she was gone. Left a note saying she wouldn't be back."

"That what it said exactly?" Carver asked.

"Yeah, it was to the point. 'Bob, I've had enough. I'm leaving and won't be back.' I remember it word for word."

"Still got the note?" —

"No, I threw it away. Saw no reason to keep it."

That didn't ring true to Carver. It was his experience that jilted spouses usually held on to such notes. A last message from someone they might never see again. Or, if the parting was bitter, tangible proof of betrayal. "She sign it?"

"Sure. Not her last name, just Elizabeth."

Carver looked at his half-empty beer can. "Like that? Her entire first name?"

"Uh-huh."

"What'd you usually call her?"

"Beth. Her friends called—call—her that, too."

"But she signed the note Elizabeth. Kinda formal. Her handwriting?"

"Yeah, I'm sure it was."

"Any reason she'd bolt?"

"Must have been. She's gone."

Mr. Wise-ass again. "I mean, that you know of. You two have an argument just before she left? Anything like that?"

For the first time Ghostly looked uneasy. He was staring at Carver with appraising dark eyes, gnawing his lower lip again but meaning it this time. "If I hire you, is what I say confidential?"

"Even if you don't," Carver assured him.

"Still . . ." Ghostly partially unwound the towel he was carrying. A leather wallet and a pair of sunglasses were cradled inside. He opened the wallet, an expensive eelskin one, and peeled out a bill. He held it out for Carver. It was a thousand-dollar bill. "I wanna make sure nothing I say gets beyond you. Want you to have some ethical obligation. Take the money. Let me be your client officially before I finish what I have to say, then you either accept the case or not, but either way you keep the thousand."

Carver was getting interested. He decided to play along. People did less for more money on TV quiz shows, didn't they? He took the bill from Ghostly's hand, folded it in quarters, and tucked it beneath the damp elastic band of his swimming trunks. He said, "You can trust me."

Ghostly said, "I know. I checked on you before I came here. You're a lot of things, Carver. Honest is one of them."

Carver didn't want to hear about the others. Better to stop with honest, while he was ahead. Settling back in the wood-and-canvas chair, hearing it creak beneath his weight, he laid his cane across his lap and stretched out his good leg alongside his bad one, the result of a bullet. Such a world.

He said, "Let's hear about Elizabeth."

| 2 |

GHOSTLY STOOD with his muscular arms crossed, his feet spread wide. He seemed more irritated than worried about his wife's disappearance. "Beth and I've been married five years," he began. Then he paused. "We're from New York originally, been living down here in Florida the past three years. Tell you the truth, both of us liked New York better. . . . "

"Almost everyone in Florida's from someplace else," Carver said, seeing Ghostly had hit a snag and didn't know what to say next. Words failed when you woke up and found a note instead of your wife. It wasn't a unique situation in the marital wars, but one that always carried impact. "If you like New York, why'd you move here?"

"My job. I was transferred. I'm a salesman for a medical supply firm, and we do business with a number of hospitals in the central and south Florida area."

"Any kids?"

Ghostly seemed oddly surprised by the question. His asymmetrical dark brows danced wildly for a moment above wide eyes, making him look almost comical. Then he calmed down. Said, "No kids. There's only me and Beth."

"You live here in Del Moray?"

"No. In Orlando."

"Think Beth went back to New York?"

"No. I mean, I don't know. It's possible."

Carver leaned back in the director's chair and studied Ghostly, whose arrogant stance didn't fit his contrite and desperate words. A medical salesman, he'd said. Salesmen came in a lot of models, but not many were openly arrogant. Obsequiousness sold, obvious arrogance didn't. Not medical supplies, anyway. He said, "You think she disliked Florida enough to leave the state?"

Ghostly shrugged, as if to say, "You're the detective."

Well, that was true. Carver said, "I'll ask again: You two have an argument before she left?"

"No, we got along."

"All the time?"

"Almost."

"She behave oddly at all in the time leading up to her leaving?"

"Oddly? No, I don't think so. That's what's puzzling me. And worrying me. Maybe she was abducted or something."

"Something?"

"Well, you know."

Carver didn't. Not exactly. But he let it pass. "So everything was going on greased rails and suddenly she jumped the tracks?"

Ghostly nodded. He uncrossed his arms and raked fingers through his thick dark hair, absently scratched his crotch. "Yeah, you could put it that way. And I'm concerned."

Carver looked out the window for a while at the blue-green, undulating ocean beyond the dead potted plants. There were a few clouds in the sky now, lying low near the horizon and riding the wind toward land. A large bird flapped past, parallel to the shore. Maybe an albatross. Carver wouldn't know; he couldn't remember ever actually seeing an albatross and wasn't sure what they looked like. Big birds, though.

"How 'bout it?" Ghostly said. "Gonna take this on and find my wife? I'd appreciate it, and I'm willing to pay generously. I've got money saved, and I can't think of a better use for it.''

''Why don't you let your tax dollars work for you, contact the police and tell them what you told me?''

Ghostly placed his fists on his hips and looked distraught. ''I told you, she left a note. To the police, she's not a missing person. They wouldn't be interested. But I'm her husband, and I don't think Beth'd just up and leave that way. And even if she did, I wanna find her, talk to her.''

Easy enough to understand. And what was Carver going to do with his days if he didn't take on the task of searching for Elizabeth Ghostly? Swim in the mornings—then what? His lady love, Edwina Talbot, was away at a real-estate convention in Atlanta. Which was one reason why Carver was here at his beach cottage, instead of at her home up the coast, where he usually stayed. The other reason was that Edwina had been acting oddly herself lately. They'd had an intimate but strangely independent relationship for the past several years, with space to breathe for each of them. No commitment.

Last week Edwina had asked for that commitment, and Carver had waffled. Since then she'd kept her distance from him, both physically and emotionally. He wasn't ready for another marriage.

He said, ''I'll look for your wife, Mr. Ghostly. I'll need some more facts. And her photograph, the most recent you have.''

Ghostly grinned and said, ''I watch TV detective shows, so I know how it works. I brought a photo with me.'' He reached into the still-folded towel he'd set on the floor, came up with a plastic-coated snapshot, and handed it to Carver.

Carver laid the photograph on his bare thigh and stared down at it, surprised to see that Elizabeth Ghostly was a black woman. A beautiful black woman. She had high, wide cheekbones, lively dark eyes, a sculpted nose, and full, pouty lips. She was wearing what looked like a cocktail dress that allowed for more than a glimpse of cleavage, had pearl earrings, and wore around her neck a string of pearls that contrasted with her dark skin. Behind her were a wall and an ornate door, and several men in tuxedos. They looked more like bouncers than headwaiters.

"That was taken six months ago at a sales convention in Miami," Ghostly said. "The Doral Hotel."

"She's an attractive woman," Carver said.

Ghostly looked proud for a moment, but still with the undercurrent of arrogance. His principal possession had been complimented. Then he seemed to remember she was missing, and he frowned.

Carver said, "Sometimes interracial marriages suffer stress. Cause one of the partners to break and leave. Any of that kinda thing in your marriage? I mean, central Florida isn't New York."

"Well, there was a little of what I guess you'd call discrimination against her—us. Some whispers at the condominium project where we live. But that died down and didn't bother either of us. And now Beth isn't even the only black woman living at Beau Capri."

"Beau Capri?"

"Yeah. That's the condo development. Right near the Orange Blossom Trail."

Carver used his cane to raise himself to his feet. He limped over to the breakfast counter, thumping the cane on the floor, and made his way around behind the counter. After fishing in a drawer for paper and pencil, he said, "Better give me as detailed a description of your wife as possible."

Ghostly seemed to enjoy doing that, pacing absently, hands on hips, as he talked: "She's thirty-three, kinda tall, and, well, you know, very nicely built. Dresses well, too."

"Any distinguishing marks? Scars or whatever?"

"Uh, yeah. About a five-inch scar on her stomach. From some sort of operation she had before we met."

Carver found it strange that Ghostly didn't know what kind of operation. "She got family in New York?"

"No, she's alone. Her family's all dead."

Carver stared at him, then jotted that information next to Beth Ghostly's physical description. "Any habits? Hobbies? Anything that could give some hint of where she mighta gone?''

"She likes dancing,'' Ghostly said. "Good times, that kinda thing. Not like she's wild, though. Not looking for action, if you know what I mean. She just likes her fun.'' He added defensively, "Nothing wrong with that.''

"She take any money when she left?''

"Not more'n a couple hundred dollars. Woman like Beth, she doesn't need money to have fun.''

"What kinda food does she like?''

"Huh?''

"Food,'' Carver said. "People get on the run, go underground, they still tend to frequent restaurants that serve their favorite food. One way to track them down.''

"If you can find out what city she's in.''

"Yeah, that comes first,'' Carver said.

Ghostly gazed up at the ceiling, thinking. "She likes Italian food best, I'd say. Pasta. Never puts on any weight, though. Amazing.''

"She use drugs? Anything like that?''

Ghostly's face reddened beneath the tan. He seemed enraged that Carver would suggest such a thing. "Maybe I gave the wrong impression. She's not that kind, Carver, believe me.''

"So give me some kinda handle, Mr. Ghostly. Someplace specific where she might turn up. There's lots of Italian restaurants and places to dance in Florida.''

Ghostly put on a helpless look and raised his shoulders in a futile shrug. "Guess it seems odd, you live with a woman over five years and it's hard to fill somebody in on that kinda thing. But we spent a lotta time together, in places that didn't serve pasta or play music. I mean, Beth likes her fun, but she's also a sorta stay-at-home type. Loves to read.''

Woman of contrasts. "Read what?''

"Hey, I dunno. I'm not much of a reader myself. She'd usually have her nose in a magazine or a book, is all I know. Liked novels written by people I never heard of.''

"She get them from the library or buy them?''

"Bought them.''

Carver said, "Okay, that's something."

Ghostly rubbed the underside of his jaw with his thumb and forefinger, as if testing to see if he needed a shave. He suddenly seemed uncomfortable. Carver didn't help him out, but instead sat staring at him. His move. His game, in fact.

Finally Ghostly took a deep breath. "Okay, there's some stuff I'm not telling you."

"You want me to find her," Carver said, "it'll be easier and faster if I know it all."

"All, huh?" Ghostly shifted his weight to his other leg. Then he stood more loosely. He seemed to have reached a decision about opening up to Carver, trusting him. "I wasn't quite straight with you on a few of my answers, Carver."

"I got that impression."

"The big reason I came here instead of to the police is Beth's habit."

"Drugs?" Well, what else—in Florida, with the wife of a medical supply salesman? Fingernail-chewing?

Ghostly actually looked ready to sob. He blew out a long breath, flapping his lips the way horses do when they're winded. "There's doctors who use heroin to treat certain diseases, as a painkiller for patients sometimes in the final stages. Anyway, there are legal, medical uses for the stuff, if it's prescribed by a physician. I sold it. And even with the careful controls kept on it, I found out about a year ago that Beth's been pilfering it from my supplies. She confessed to me she was addicted."

"You get her any help?"

"Treatment? I tried like hell, but she wouldn't agree to it. She's . . . well, she's ashamed."

"So you've been supplying her on the sly."

"Yeah. Not much, though. And just before she left me, she'd agreed to use methadone, and if that didn't work she'd check into a drug rehab clinic."

Now Carver understood how it might have gone. The wife knowing she was even more deeply hooked than her husband thought. Knowing, or believing, that she was on the long slide and there was no way off. Maybe she'd left him because he couldn't understand. Maybe she didn't want him to see her ride her habit all the way to the grave. She'd had reasons for running, had Beth Ghostly.

There was little arrogance in Ghostly now. It had cost him, telling Carver this about his wife, and placed him in some jeopardy, too; supplying an addict, even a spouse, with a controlled substance was a crime. Technically, Carver was supposed to report it. Only the fact that Ghostly would deny their conversation kept him from even considering that ethical dilemma. The best thing all around would be for Beth to return to her husband and get treatment for her addiction, maybe have a chance. Some hell to live through, but a chance.

Carver said, "She get narcotics anywhere except from you?"

"Well, I guess I better be honest all the way. I think she did buy from someone else. I have no idea who, or where she got the stuff. My only reason for thinking it is that there's no way she could have become so heavily addicted on what little I gave her. No way." His eyes teared up. "I mean, Jesus, Carver, she'd beg for it! Do anything for it! It made me fucking sick!" He turned away for a moment to compose himself, then turned back slowly. His face was pale. "It still makes me ill to think about it," he said.

"And now she's out there with only a few hundred dollars."

"Well, more than that. I lied about how much she left with. Last week I went to my bank and found she'd withdrawn exactly half our savings."

"Amounting to?"

"Nearly ten thousand dollars."

"Enough to keep her in dope for a while, if she makes a connection and finds a dealer."

"The ten thousand won't last long, the habit she has. And a user by herself in that world, they'll take every advantage of her. That's something that scares hell outa me."

Carver sat staring at the photograph for a while, then looked up. "So I'll look into it," he said, as if it were no big deal and he hadn't been sitting there carefully weighing whether to get involved. "Where can I get in touch with you?"

"I won't be at our condo for a week or so," Ghostly said. "A convention down in Miami I can't skip without fear of losing employment." He worked his out-of-whack eyebrows fearfully. "Christ, that'd be the kicker, if I lost my job on top of the rest of this mess."

Carver said, "Go to your convention. If I need more information I'll phone you at your hotel."

"Fine. It's the Holiday Inn on Collins." He lurched forward and shook Carver's hand again. This time there was unsteadiness in his grip, and not much strength. "Find her, Carver, please."

Carver said, "I'll be working at it. Any of your neighbors Beth was particularly thick with?"

"Not really. We kept pretty much to ourselves. And I traveled most of the time."

Carver disengaged his right hand from Ghostly's. He said he wanted Ghostly to sign a standard contract before he left, then answer a few more questions. Ghostly agreed immediately, and Carver limped to his dresser behind the folding screen and got a contract from the middle drawer.

Ghostly scrawled his signature, set down the pen, and said again, "Find her." More prayer than request.

"If I can't find her," Carver said, "she'll still need to be found. Still need help. Will you agree to go to the police when I tell you I'm wasting your money?"

Ghostly said, "I thought that out carefully before I walked in here. The answer's yes."

Carver gave him his copy of the contract. "I'll do what I can to see that doesn't happen, Mr. Ghostly."

Ghostly submitted himself to another ten minutes of question-and-answer. Then he managed a thin grin and walked from the cottage, leaving behind to linger whatever it was that had aroused uneasiness in Carver when he'd approached him on the beach.

Maybe it was the uneasiness, and his curiosity, that had

really prompted Carver to take the case. That and the money.

And a young woman out there alone somewhere, running and bedeviled.

3

THE BEAU CAPRI condominiums didn't look remotely French. As Carver steered his ancient Olds convertible onto the azalea-bordered driveway of the parking lot, he saw a series of three-story buildings constructed of vertical slabs of cast concrete, with what appeared to be seashells embedded in them. The flat roofs had air-conditioning units mounted on them, surrounded by symmetrical, blunt-tipped picket fences that looked as if they ought to be on the ground and not three stories in the air. Set in the middle of the four buildings was the ubiquitous swimming pool, this one as unimaginative as the rest of the architecture. A rectangular pool with high and low diving boards, a wide concrete apron, and uncomfortable-looking nylon-webbed chairs and lounges. The whole bland creation was surrounded by a chain-link fence coated with some sort of pastel pink rubber Carver had never seen before. Voltaire would have defended to his death the residents' right to live in Beau Capri, but he would never have moved in himself.

The drive from Del Moray to the Orlando area had taken only about an hour on sun-washed highways, and it wasn't yet noon. Carver had driven in with the Olds's canvas top down, letting the wind whip around him and try to mess up hair no longer on his head. A small and bitter triumph over nature.

He parked the Olds at the far end of the lot, alongside a low red Porsche. After killing the powerful V-8 engine, he listened for a moment to cooling metal ticking beneath the long hood. Most of the cars in the lot were expensive; the dented and rusty Olds looked like a wino who'd crashed a swank party.

Carver checked addresses emblazoned on the visible sides of each building and saw that the Ghostly unit would be in the extreme left building, on the third floor. As he climbed out of the Olds, heat from beneath the car wafted out and embraced his ankles. He set his cane on the sun-warmed concrete and began limping toward the sidewalk that flanked the pool's pink fence.

There were a few kids splashing around in the pool. Also an old man with a chest thick with gray hair and gold medallions. A lean and beautifully built woman about fifty, in a scanty black bikini, stood hipshot near the fence. She had platinum blond hair, skin the color of burnt toast, and sharp white teeth, which she showed as she glanced at Carver and either grimaced or smiled—he wasn't sure which.

"Help you?"

An elderly, gray-haired man with a huge stomach paunch was blocking Carver's way on the sidewalk. He wore dark slacks and a white short-sleeved shirt with some sort of insignia on one shoulder. Low-key but alert security. Apparently people didn't simply walk into Beau Capri. If it wasn't exclusive, what was it selling?

Carver flashed his reassuring, beatific smile, in surprising contrast to the harshness of his features. "I'm looking for the Ghostlys' condo. It's in that end building, they said."

"That's right." The old man's faded blue eyes had narrowed. He was measuring Carver, staying affable but suspicious, in the manner of security guards. He tugged his belt up on his right hip, as if he was used to having a gun there. A former cop, maybe. "Mind if I ask the nature of your business, sir?"

"I'm not a pesky salesman," Carver said.

The old guy said, "Didn't figure."

Carver drew out his wallet and showed his ID.

"Private, huh?" the guard said. "Ghostlys got some kinda trouble?"

"Maybe. Seen Mrs. Ghostly lately?"

"Not in a while. But that ain't unusual, what with the baby and all."

"Baby?"

He brushed aside a mosquito that had been droning around his eyes in defiance of authority. "Sure. She's pregnant as hell. Been that way for about eight months."

Here was something Bob Ghostly hadn't mentioned. Carver leaned on his cane. He felt something cold slink up his spine. "We talking about the same Elizabeth Ghostly?"

" 'Magine so. Husband name of Robert. One nice gal. Well liked around here, even though she does tend to keep to herself. Got her reasons, I expect."

"What kinda reasons?"

"Oh, they'd be personal, I'm sure."

"I noticed you didn't say hubby was well liked."

The guard seemed to consider leveling with Carver. A warm breeze ruffled his white hair, rattled the palm fronds overhead. He said, " 'Tween you and me, hubby's a prick. Acts like he owns this place and everyone in it."

"Really?" Carver feigned surprise. "He told me he was hardly ever here. Said he traveled around selling medical supplies."

"Yeah, he's gone mosta the time, but when he's here he expects folks to get outa his way. Beth Ghostly, now, she'll always stop and talk to the other residents. They was cool to her at first, her being black and all, but once they got to know her they had no choice but to like her. Most everyone here's interested in her pregnancy. Lotsa folks figure she disappeared 'cause she went into labor, maybe had the baby. Couple of people tried to ask her husband, but he just ignored them and hurried on about his business. Always in a major fuckin' rush, that one. Important man on the run. Or so he sees himself."

Carver considered telling the guard Bob Ghostly had hired him and that Beth was missing, but he decided not to get the residents all excited and gossiping. The main reason Ghostly had come to him instead of going to the law was to keep the investigation low-profile.

He handed the guard one of his cards. "Maybe she did have that baby. I'll let you know. Meanwhile, will you give me a call if you see her?"

"Sure." The guard slipped the card into his shirt pocket. "You don't figure . . . well, I shouldn't ask this. I mean, why you're working for the Ghostlys is none of my business, and I guess you wouldn't tell me if I asked."

Carver said, "That's right. Client confidentiality."

"I'm curious, though. There some kinda trouble between Beth and her husband?"

"No reason to think that."

The guard smiled. He'd have thought less of Carver if he'd gotten an answer.

Sweat was trickling down Carver's ribs and the inside of his right arm. "I'll go on up to their unit now," he said, "if it's okay with you."

"Sure," the guard said, stepping completely off the walk and onto the thick grass to let the cripple pass. "Hope there's no kinda trouble for Beth Ghostly, though."

"I hope so, too," Carver said, meaning it. He limped through glaring sunlight toward the pale, far building.

GHOSTLY HADN'T supplied him with a key, but that was okay. Cheap apartment locks gave easily to Carver's honed Visa card. Only dead-bolt locks frustrated him, but most of the time they were mounted on interior doors separately, above the main knob and lock.

Carver had the door unlocked in less than a minute. He shoved it open and noticed immediately that the air was stale and motionless. Warm, too. The thermostat had been set to Off or turned up.

He planted the tip of his cane and moved inside, then stood braced on the cane in the condo's spacious living room and glanced around.

The place was wall-to-wall glitz, but expensive glitz.

Ghostly must do better than all right selling medical supplies. The carpet was lavender, the ceiling-to-floor drapes cream-colored with bright flecks that matched the carpet. The wallpaper was fuzzy, white cardboardlike stuff shot through with silver that appeared to be real metal.

The furniture was made up of leather and glass and sharp angles of stainless steel. A long, low sofa dominated the room, white leather with gleaming steel arms, crowded with a scattering of lavender throw pillows. In front of it was a steel-framed coffee table with a glass top and glassed-in sides. The glass-enclosed cubicle contained an ornate and colorful arrangement of plastic flowers and fake butterflies. The wide window's drapes were open, admitting brilliant sunlight that made the wallpaper glitter. There were several chrome-framed oil paintings on the wall. One of them was of a bullfighter victoriously holding high the slain bull's severed ears while an array of flowers and hats rained down on him from an admiring crowd. The bullfighter was wearing a crooked grin and looked a bit like Bob Ghostly.

Carver limped across the living room to a hall that led toward what he presumed was the bedroom, noticing there was a thin, almost imperceptible layer of dust over everything, which robbed it of truly eye-aching luster. He glanced in the bathroom and saw a maroon hot tub for two, a washbasin shaped like a flower, gold plumbing. The wallpaper in there was fuzzy, too. It had a fleur-de-lis design. Hey, French!

No wallpaper in the bedroom, but it was painted a pale rose and all the furniture was white. The bed was round with a white spread and resembled a huge mushroom that had sprung up from the carpet. Carver went to it and rested a palm on it. The wide expanse of spread undulated; a water bed. He glanced up and saw himself. A mirrored ceiling. Sure.

His cane left quarter-size depressions in the thick rose carpet as he limped toward the mirrored closet doors. He shoved the nearer door open on its rollers and saw men's suits and sport coats. A lot of them, and of good quality. The closet was set up with those white wire shelves and drawers for maximum use of space. One shelf contained half a dozen pairs of men's shoes, all of them black except for a pair of gray Etonic joggers with thick white soles.

Carver slid the door closed smoothly on its growling rollers, then opened the other door.

Beth's side of the closet. Dresses, silky blouses, a pair of designer jeans on a slacks hanger. High-heeled shoes on the shelf that corresponded to her husband's shoe shelf. Size seven and a half. Expensive brands.

Carver limped to the dresser and carefully searched through its drawers. Silk lingerie, folded slacks, one drawer containing nothing but panty hose. Bras in a middle drawer; Carver couldn't help but notice they were size 36-D. In the top drawer was a white leather jewelry box full of what looked like genuine stuff that had to be worth a small fortune. Maybe a large fortune. Folded next to the padded box was a cheap white T-shirt with one of those yellow smiley faces on it. There was a gory bullet hole in Smiley's forehead, from which ran a trickle of blood. Carver was glad he'd found the T-shirt; it somehow humanized Beth Ghostly. Everything else in the apartment seemed to belong to a Saks mannequin who used the place to store goodies between jobs posing in show windows.

The atmosphere in the bedroom was so stifling that Carver considered finding the thermostat and setting it so the air conditioner came on. Then he decided he wasn't going to be here much longer. He limped back toward the living room, making not a sound on the deep carpet.

He was standing in the living room and taking a last look around when he happened to glance out the window. It looked out over the parking lot. On the curved sidewalk, near where Carver had talked with the security guard, a black woman was standing and talking with a woman in a red bathing suit. From up here the palm fronds partially blocked his view and he couldn't tell what either woman looked like; he remembered Ghostly saying there were other black residents in Beau Capri now.

Carver moved back from the window and was about to leave the condo when he decided he might as well use the bathroom. It seemed a shame to let all that gold plumbing sit idle.

He'd just finished relieving himself, and was about to flush the toilet, when he heard a noise from the living room. Not loud, but it sounded like the door closing.

He zipped his fly and backed away from the commode.

Moving close to the door, he found an angle of vision that allowed him to see about half of the living room. The garish glass coffee table. Part of the low white sofa with its lineup of throw pillows.

He caught a flicker of shadow and pressed his body back just in time not to be seen by the woman who hurried down the hall to the bedroom, leaving in her wake a strong perfume scent that smelled like roses. She hadn't glanced in the bathroom, and Carver had caught only a glimpse of her. He didn't think she was Beth Ghostly. She had on a dark skirt and a blue sleeveless blouse. He thought she was probably the black woman he'd seen standing and talking on the sidewalk below the window.

As he was considering sneaking out while she was occupied in the bedroom, the smooth scraping noises of drawers opening and closing came to him. Something about the sounds suggested a certain familiarity; there was a hurried sureness about them that implied the woman was in her own bedroom. Maybe this *was* Elizabeth Ghostly. Photographs could deceive.

He decided to confront the woman, whoever she was, but not quite yet. He eased out into the hall, catching a glimpse of her. She had her back to him, leaning over the bed and stuffing clothes into a suitcase. Dark arms, lean waist and flared hips.

Carver limped into the living room and stood against the wall by the door, partially concealed by a curio cabinet cluttered with Hummel figurines and crystal birds. A glass owl stared knowingly at him as he waited for the woman to emerge from the bedroom.

Almost five minutes had crawled past on Carver's Seiko watch when she trudged out carrying two matching red suitcases that were obviously heavy. The scent of roses came with her. She was tall, maybe five-ten, thin-limbed but busty, and perspiring heavily from her efforts in the warm bedroom. She wasn't Elizabeth Ghostly; her features were broader and her eyes smaller and more deeply set. She had on very red lipstick that looked wet.

She put the suitcases down, still not seeing Carver, and wiped the back of her hand across her glistening forehead. Said, ''Holy Jesus!'' apparently commenting to herself on the heat, and walked over to the window. A graceful walk, now that she wasn't burdened by the suitcases. She glanced out the window in all directions, as if to make sure no one was out there waiting for her.

Then she turned around and saw Carver.

Shock hollowed her out; the vacuum caused an intake of breath that shrieked in the quiet room.

Carver limped across the spongy carpet, smiling and holding his free hand at eye level and palm out, as if about to recite the Boy Scout oath. He didn't want the woman to have a heart attack. He actually said, ''Now, don't be alarmed.''

Fear crossed her face, widened and brightened her eyes. Then anger washed in. She seemed to encourage the anger, much preferring it to terror.

She said, ''Jus' who the fuck—'' and the side of her head exploded.

4

CARVER LAY curled on his side on the carpet, where he'd dropped automatically once he realized the woman had been shot.

His cheek pressed flat against the rough fibers, he glanced over and saw her lying spraddle-legged on the floor, her skirt bunched up around her hips. Her bowels had released. The ruined side of her head was turned away from him. *Thanks for that!* There was a wide smear of blood and gray brain matter on the wall, like horrifying modern art. What looked like a tiny black hairpiece with something shiny and white poking through it lay beneath the smear, near the baseboard. Carver saw a dark pattern of blood on his shirt and bare right forearm and felt his stomach lurch. He swallowed a taste bitter and metallic. Almost gagged.

What now? It was quiet outside and in the condo. Mingled with the stench of feces, he caught a whiff of roses. The dead woman's perfume. He felt shaky.

Jesus, he was hot! He swiveled his head in sudden alarm and was relieved to find he was low enough that no one could see him through the window; the gunman might still be out there, finger on the trigger.

Might. But Carver was pretty sure the killer had gotten away as soon as possible after accomplishing his mission.

People didn't tend to hang around murder scenes if they were the perpetrator.

The cane was on the floor, near the woman's sprawled body. Carver stretched out an arm for it, closed fingers on the crook of hard walnut, and pulled it toward him. He felt immediately better, whole and more secure now.

Still staying low, he used the cane for support and worked himself into a sitting position. He scooted away from the window, but not before seeing the single round bullet hole in the thick thermal glass. It was just left of center in the middle pane; it had turned the glass milky but none of it had fallen from its metal frame. Safety glass, but not safe enough for the woman on the floor.

Not looking at the dead woman, Carver crawled awkwardly to the window, his shoe making a scraping sound as his bad leg dragged behind him on the carpet. He peeked outside, around the fold of the drape.

Several people were milling around below, including the old security guard who'd stopped and questioned him on the way to the condo. They'd heard the shot, though in his rush of shock *he* hadn't, even though he'd been standing next to the victim. He remembered hearing only the sickening impact of the bullet.

The curious and remotely alarmed folks below were craning their necks, peering this way and that to determine where the noise had originated. Sooner or later one of them would notice the milky window in the third-floor unit, and realize that what they'd heard might indeed have been what it sounded like: gunfire. He drew the drapes closed.

Carver made his way across the rough carpet to the phone. The effort was hard on his good knee, of which he took exceptional care. He pulled the desk-model white phone down to him; it dinged when it struck the floor. Leaning his back against the wall, he depressed the cradle button a few times to make sure he had a dial tone. Then he made two phone calls.

The first was to the Holiday Inn on Collins in Miami. He was told there was no convention of medical suppliers there, nor was one scheduled. No Robert or Bob Ghostly was registered there, either.

So much for loyalty to the client.

Carver's second call was to Lieutenant Alfonso Desoto of the Orlando police department.

CARVER SAT on the low white leather sofa with the stainless-steel arms, comfortable as a cat on a fence top. Someone had thought to turn the air conditioning on and the condo wasn't so warm, but he was still sweating.

The ME was finished with the body, but the evidence team was still bustling about in its murmuring, controlled way. Vacuuming, photographing, dusting for prints. Establishing facts if not some sort of logic that might explain the carnage. The hope was that logic and pattern would emerge later, spawned by meticulous attention to minutiae.

Desoto finished talking to the departing ME, then he walked over to stand near Carver. A tall man with broad shoulders and a waspish waist, he was as darkly handsome as a Hollywood bullfighter. Tailored cream-colored suit, white shirt, mauve tie, oxblood shoes that looked made for dancing. He smiled down at Carver, teeth carnivorous white perfection against his smooth tan complexion. His wavy black hair, impeccably combed as always, shone in the shaft of light beaming through the crack left by the drapes that didn't quite meet. Dust motes swirled in the slanted golden ray, stirred up by police activity.

Irritated by Desoto's smile, Carver said, "Not a fucking thing I can think's funny about this."

Desoto shrugged, but his dashing smile lost candle-power. "I was just considering all the shit you get yourself into, *amigo*. It's amazing."

Carver took that kind of observation from Desoto without rancor or firing back a smartass answer. They'd been friends for years, since Carver's days in the department. They knew each other layers deep. Desoto had goaded Carver to stay in police work, become a private investigator instead of a self-pitying beach bum. There were no hard feelings except from time to time, when it wasn't lost on Carver that, on average, beach bums outlived private cops.

Neither man said anything as two white-uniformed attendants fitted the corpse into a black rubber body bag. Zipped the bag noisily with a ratchety sound that sawed through Carver, then eased it onto a gurney that was raised with a lot of metallic clicking as its mechanism locked it into place. The gurney had large, chrome-spoked rubber wheels. One of them made a faint, rhythmic squeaking noise as the attendants rolled their grisly burden across the carpet and out the door. Out in the hall, the attendants began discussing where they'd have lunch. This was all a normal day's work for everyone involved. Well, not everyone. The day hadn't been normal for the woman in the bag.

Desoto waited till the last of the evidence team had left. The door to the hall remained open. A tan-uniformed elbow was visible, and a black-holstered revolver with a checkered butt. A uniform was standing guard in the hall but was well beyond earshot of Carver and Desoto.

Desoto carefully unbuttoned his suit coat, revealing a thick gold tie clasp. He was wearing a gold watch, a gold-link bracelet on his other wrist, a gold ring on each hand. He liked gold almost as much as he liked clothes. Sitting down carefully on the opposite end of the sofa, he crossed his legs slowly and without much pressure, so he wouldn't mash the creases in his pants. He said, "I think I better know about this in detail, my friend."

And Carver told him everything, in detail. This was a homicide case and not an occasion to play cute.

WHEN CARVER was finished talking, Desoto stood up slowly and stretched. He tucked his shirt back in neatly and smoothed nonexistent wrinkles from the tropical weave material of his pants, then buttoned his suit coat and walked over to the milky window. He gazed outside through a clear section of glass, his back to Carver, looking like a soap-opera star striking a pose.

He said, "Place still smells like death, eh?"

"Yeah. You should be used to that smell."

"Both of us, *amigo*."

Carver didn't say anything. Waited.

When he turned around, Desoto said, "The dead woman's driver's license gave an address in Indianapolis. Her name was Belinda Jackson."

Carver said, "I don't make a connection. Never heard the name."

"This Ghostly guy never mentioned it?"

"Nope."

"So Belinda Jackson wasn't his wife? By Ghostly or any other name?"

Carver reached into his shirt pocket, drew out Beth Ghostly's photograph, and held it out so Desoto could look at it. Desoto leaned very close to peer at the snapshot, making Carver wonder if his old pal had reached the age where he needed glasses. Desoto would be the last to admit it; he'd probably go to contacts on the sly.

But he saw the photo well enough. "Not the dead woman," he said. He tilted the photo at a slight angle. "A beauty, eh? Cheekbones like a movie star's."

There wasn't much Desoto didn't notice about women. And women paid the same studious attention to him.

Carver rotated the tip of his cane on the soft carpet, making a deep depression, and waited for Desoto to continue.

Desoto unbuttoned his suit coat and slid his hands in his pants pocket. Poised and casual as a male model. He said, "If this guy Ghostly contacts you again, let me know, eh?"

"You'll be my first phone call," Carver told him. He didn't like what he'd stepped into. Wanted out. Wanted to stay honest and alive. He suspected those goals might not be compatible.

"I guess what you're thinking," Desoto said, "is that the shooter might have been aiming at you."

"It entered my mind." *Better than the way a bullet entered Belinda Jackson's mind.* He planted the cane more firmly in the deep depression in the carpet and raised himself up from the low sofa. "But I kinda doubt it. Such a perfect fatal shot. Be a real coincidence if a miss did such a thorough job on the person next to the intended target.''

"You're probably right, *amigo*. Hope so, anyway.'' He removed his left hand from his pocket and rotated his wrist to glance at his watch. Gold cuff links glittered, causing light to dance over the wall near the bloodstain. "Tell you what, give me a while to gather and coordinate what we're finding out about this initially. Come by the office this afternoon, say about three o'clock, sign a statement, and we'll see if we can make any sense outa all this, right?''

"Sounds sensible,'' Carver said. "I'll go to a motel. Wash off what I can of what happened here. Howard Johnson's on the Orange Blossom Trail. I'll call you if I can't get a room there and wind up someplace else.''

"Fine,'' Desoto said. Concern deepened his large dark eyes. "You want some temporary protection?''

"No. The key word's *temporary*.''

" 'Fraid you're right.''

Desoto walked toward the door, his expensive suit moving like a second, silky skin. He paused and glanced back at Carver. "Leaving? Or are you feeling at home by now?''

"Leaving,'' Carver said. "I've read all the magazines.''

"Bet not the ones on the back of the closet shelf,'' Desoto said.

Carver didn't know what he meant by that, and didn't ask. He'd decided to let the resources of the law fit available puzzle pieces together, then he'd garner whatever information Desoto would share later at headquarters.

As he limped toward where Desoto waited at the door, he couldn't keep from looking at the dark stain on the carpet. Seeing again the left side of Belinda Jackson's head gushing outward. Hearing again the melon-solid *thwump!* of the high-velocity bullet smashing through bone and brain matter in thousandths of a second. Still so vivid, all of it. In dying color. Death wasn't something off in the distance, gradually drawing nearer so we could be ready for it. Death jumped at us unexpectedly out of bright sunlight.

In the hall Desoto reminded him: "Three o'clock, *amigo*."

Carver said he could hardly wait. Which was a wisecrack to help hold the horror at bay, but also true.

5

DESOTO'S OFFICE was cool. His window unit that supplemented the central air was toiling away, gurgling and humming with gusto so that the yellow ribbons tied to its grillwork were perfectly horizontal, rigid and trembling in the breeze. On the sill of the window next to the air conditioner sat Desoto's portable Sony radio. When Carver limped into the office, Desoto swiveled in his desk chair and turned down the volume. A female vocalist's lilting Spanish lament became faint; the drums of the band backing her up continued to throb like a heartbeat through the office.

Desoto laid aside a yellow file folder whose contents he'd been reading. He flashed his dashing smile and motioned elegantly for Carver to sit down in the ladder-backed oak chair in front of the desk.

Carver positioned his cane, leaned on it for support, and sat. The chair creaked beneath the sudden descent of his weight.

"Still hot outside?" Desoto asked. He was wearing his suit coat and had his mauve tie firmly knotted. He looked a long way from breaking a sweat.

"What do you care?" Carver asked. "You're never bothered by the heat."

Desoto said, "All mental, *amigo*. You wanna talk about the weather, or about the Jackson woman's murder?"

"Murder," Carver said, not bothering to mention it was Desoto who'd brought up the subject of the weather.

Desoto leaned back but kept his hands on the desk, causing his coat sleeves to ride up slightly so his cuff links glinted in the light angling through the mini-blinds. "Victim was Belinda Louella Jackson of Indianapolis. Age thirty-five, employed as a cocktail waitress. The slug that killed her was a .30-06, fired from the roof of one of the buildings that angles so it allows a clear shot through the window. Gravel on the roof was disturbed where the gunman had sat or kneeled to take aim. No ejected casing, though. If there was one, whoever shot Belinda Jackson took the time and trouble to pick up the shell before ducking through a service passage from the roof and fleeing down the fire stairs."

"One shot. No casing. Sounds like a professional."

"Yeah. No doubt used a scope. There's a mark on the roof tiles where he probably rested the barrel for support. Wanted the rifle steady because he knew he'd probably only have one shot."

Carver said, "Learn anything else about the dead woman?"

"Several things. Among them, she was the sister of the woman who lives there."

Carver folded both hands on the crook of his cane and leaned forward in his chair. "Jackson was Elizabeth Ghostly's maiden name?"

"Elizabeth Gomez's," Desoto said.

Carver said, "Explain."

"There is no Elizabeth Ghostly. No Robert Ghostly, either. But there's a Roberto Gomez, and he fits your client's description. This Roberto Gomez, *amigo,* he gave you a line of shit. But you're not the first. I been talking with the Miami Police; Gomez is a drug kingpin in southern Florida. Has connections in South America and deals any kinda stuff he can wholesale. Got houses and apartments all over the place. Only one the Miami police or DEA say they *didn't* know about was the condo here in

Orlando, where he had his wife Elizabeth stashed the past eight months.''

"Because she was pregnant,'' Carver said, "and he wanted her out of any danger because of his business.''

"You're speculating.''

"Yeah, I know.''

"And you accuse *me* of being a romantic.''

"You are. And maybe Gomez is, too.''

"Most likely. His wife's pregnancy's another thing the authorities in south Florida didn't know about Gomez.''

"Tell me some of what they *do* know.''

"He's second-generation American, of Cuban descent. His father was a burglar in New York, shot to death by police nine years ago. Gomez got into narcotics trafficking up east. Arrested three times for dealing, convicted once. Did four years at Attica. Earned a reputation as a bad-ass up there. Tough con who ran his cellblock.''

It was difficult for Carver to reconcile this description with the ordinary, cocky little man who'd passed himself off as a medical supply salesman. Medical supplies, all right. He'd flirted with the truth when he said he sold heroin. "Any warrants out for Gomez?'' Carver asked.

Desoto shook his head no. "He's gotten clever since he's moved south. Miami Narcotics and the Drug Enforcement Administration keep a watch on him, though, waiting for him to screw up. They know he's one of Florida's major dealers, but they need more than they got if they wanna prove it in court. He's also one ruthless cookie, *amigo*. He's got a longtime lieutenant name of Hirsh does the mean work. Gomez enjoys watching, they tell me. But he's still capable of most anything himself. He doesn't do drugs and he doesn't allow any of his employees to use the stuff. Last year, in the Keys, he found out one of his men was carrying a habit. Gomez cut off the guy's fingertips with a machete and towed him behind the boat. Got a charge outa what happened when sharks were attracted by the blood.''

"No proof, though?'' Carver asked.

Desoto smiled faintly. "Not unless you can get sharks

to testify. DEA knows who else was on the boat, but no-body's talking.''

Carver couldn't blame them. Seeing sharks make a meal of one of your co-workers would stick in the mind and prompt loyalty to the employer.

"So what we have," Desoto said, "is Gomez wanders up to you on the beach, pretends to be someone else, and hires you to find his wife."

"His real wife," Carver said.

"So far, anyway. But he neglects to tell you she's pregnant."

"She might have already had the baby," Carver pointed out.

"True. Nobody knows how pregnant she is—or was. Anyway, you go to the address Gomez gives you—where he actually did spend time with his wife and where she's been more or less living much of the past year—and the wife's sister walks in and gets shot by a sniper." Desoto leaned back into the breeze from the window unit. His wavy dark hair didn't budge in the flow of air. "*Amigo*, tell me what it all means."

Carver had been sitting there wondering exactly that. He said, "Well, I don't think I was used to set up Gomez's sister-in-law. It doesn't connect. She must have arrived at the apartment unexpectedly."

"Uh-huh. But why, do you figure?"

"To get some clothes and personal items for her sister, who's in hiding."

"Hiding from?"

"I don't know. Gomez?"

"Maybe from Gomez. But I don't think so. And the unfortunate Belinda Jackson?"

"Shot by mistake," Carver said. "Because the killer, firing from a distance, thought she was Elizabeth Gomez."

"That's how it coulda been, all right." Desoto sat forward again. He placed his elbows on his desk and clasped his neat, tanned hands together. "What if somebody's trying to kill Elizabeth Gomez, and hubby Roberto wants to find her so he can protect her, eh?"

"That the way you're leaning?"

"For now, *amigo*."

"She's more likely running *from* Gomez, which is why he hired me to find her."

"Except he stashed her out of harm's way in the Orlando condo to begin with. My impression is he was trying to protect her and the baby they were expecting."

"Then Gomez really thinks somebody snatched her—or them," Carver said. "According to your hypothesis."

"It falls that way," Desoto said. "An abduction."

Carver considered it. Didn't like it. Didn't say anything.

Desoto said, "By the bye, sooner or later a DEA agent name of Dan Strait will wanna talk to you. He's naturally interested in anything concerning Gomez."

"Reasonable."

"Considering what happened, you probably won't see Gomez again. But if you do, let me know. It's not just the DEA that wants a word with him."

"You see him as a suspect?"

"Oh, no. Even if he shot the woman, he'll have an alibi a team of high-powered lawyers couldn't budge in a year."

"A careful man, huh?"

"Miami tells me he's awful nifty as well as psychotic. DEA says the same thing. What drug money can do to people, it's done to Gomez. Guy's major-league dangerous, so you be careful yourself."

"You know me."

"Sure do, my friend. Once you get involved in something, you can't let go. Give some dogs a rag to chew on, and when they get a tooth-hold they'll tug at it till they drop. That's the way you are." He reached back and turned up the Sony's volume. A tango was playing; very dramatic. "Anything you wanna add before you go into an interrogation room and make your official statement, *amigo*?"

Carver leaned forward over the cane and stood up. He said, "Belinda Jackson was a slender, well-built woman. Even through a telescopic sight and a window, there's no way she'd look to be in the late stages of pregnancy."

"I noticed that about her," Desoto said.

"Figured you would," Carver said, and went out.

Hoping he'd never see Roberto Gomez again, but knowing better.

Dogs and rags.

6

ON THE DRIVE back to Del Moray, Carver stopped at the Happy Lobster on A1A and had a leisurely supper of crab legs washed down with draft beer. It was cool and quiet in the restaurant, making it easier to think sanely. Faint noise was drifting from the bar. Men argued good-naturedly—about what he couldn't tell. Someone coughed, a nasty cigarette hack. A woman laughed a rising, uncontrollable shriek of mirth. They were having a good time, all right.

Carver had followed the hostess farther into the restaurant, away from the noise. He sat in one of the booths by the wide, curved window and looked out at the darkening Atlantic. A couple of fishing boats were moving parallel to the shore, surrounded by gulls in the way fleas surround dogs. The clouds that had lain on the horizon that morning had been pushed in by the sea wind and turned the sky a low, leaden gray, but the temperature was still up in the nineties. It was muggy as a sauna out there. Rain ready to happen.

Carver and Edwina had shared a lot of meals at the Happy Lobster, but he didn't feel sentimental and he didn't know why. She was due back from Atlanta tonight. She might even be back now. He could have driven all the way in to her place and possibly had supper with her.

Six months ago, maybe one month ago, that's what he would have done. Shared with her what had happened with Roberto Gomez and his missing wife and dead sister-in-law. But Edwina had demanded the total commitment from him that he couldn't give. Sensing he'd never surrender a private side of himself, she'd been pushing him away, gaining emotional distance and courage for a break they both knew was coming.

Unless Carver relented and gave her marriage and all it entailed.

And he knew he never would. His marriage to Laura had soured him on the institution. It was a reaction he couldn't control; marriage was a setup for pain. Just looking at a flame could make you hurt again where you'd been burned.

He sipped his beer and gazed out at the ocean rolling in from a far part of the planet. He'd had enough of pain, seen enough of it and was undoubtedly going to see more. He wanted as little as possible of it to be his. Selfish? Maybe. Or maybe more like self-preservation. Edwina had felt the same way a few years ago, after her own disastrous marriage and rebound love affair. Since then she'd healed. Carver hadn't. That simple.

He finished his third beer, paid his check, and limped out to the parking lot, where he stood and smoked a Swisher Sweet cigar. Cars carrying the supper crowd were pulling in from the highway and parking. He listened to gravel crunching beneath tires and shoes, and watched people, usually in pairs, stride into the restaurant.

Finally he flicked the glowing cigar butt out toward the ocean, watching it streak against the gray sky and fall just on the other side of the guardrail.

Then he got in the Olds and drove to Edwina's house, where now he lived only part of the time.

HER MERCEDES, which she'd left in a park-and-fly lot at the airport, was in the driveway nosed against the closed garage door. The palm fronds overhead, swaying in the breeze, sent faint shadows over the car's roof and hood. Carver braked the Olds next to it and made plenty of noise slamming the door and dragging his cane so she'd know he was coming. As if he didn't want to surprise her with a new lover, though he was sure there wasn't one.

She'd been home awhile. She'd changed from her career-woman outfit into Levi's and a sleeveless white blouse. Her thick auburn hair, worn often in a bun these days, fell to below her shoulders. Her gray eyes surveyed him with pinpoints of pain. She looked older, as if the gloom of the evening had seeped into her mind. The strain between them was showing on her.

Seated on the living room sofa with one of the lemonade-and-gin drinks she favored, she said, "I phoned your cottage and you weren't there. Wondered where you were."

He crossed the room halfway and leaned on his cane. "Had to drive into Orlando on business."

She sipped at her spiked lemonade, then licked her lips sensuously. If he didn't know better he might have guessed she was flirting. "I thought we might go out for supper. The stuff they served on the plane tasted like plastic and I only nibbled at it."

"Wish I'd known," Carver said. "I stopped and ate on the drive back."

No change of expression. "Doesn't matter. Plenty of frozen dinners out there." She motioned with her head in the direction of the kitchen, more a direct stare and a ducking of her chin than a sideways tilt. It caused something to tighten around Carver's heart. She was beautiful when she did that; it was a gesture exclusively hers.

He limped to the wing chair and sat down, stiff leg extended in front of him, cane resting against his thigh. The heel of his moccasin was digging into the carpet. "So how'd the real-estate conference go?"

She smiled. "The way they always do. Speeches, panels, luncheons, cocktail parties. General business shmoozing. Some misbehaving by those foolish enough to mix work and play."

"Hear any more about the Hawaiian project?"

He shouldn't have asked. Tension crept like a shadow onto her face, stiffening her cheeks. Her smooth, fighter's jaw jutted farther out almost imperceptibly, but Carver noticed; he knew her moods, even if he didn't understand her completely. She said, "They're still going to build it, if that's what you mean."

"I guess that's pretty much what I meant."

She stood up too quickly, then paced in an irregular pattern over the blue carpet, holding her glass delicately as if it were brimming with liquid instead of half empty. "You know, Fred—"

"What?" He couldn't help interrupting her, and loudly. Knowing as he did so that they were too damned combative tonight. War was in the air.

She must have sensed the same mood. She said, "Nothing. What's the new case about?"

"Didn't say I had a new case."

"When I left for Atlanta, you didn't have an old one." True enough. Give her a point.

"What is it," she asked, "top secret, you don't wanna talk about it?"

"Nothing like that," he said, straight-faced. Irritated. Maybe he *was* into something he shouldn't talk about, even with her. It had happened before.

But always he'd talked with her anyway.

Not this time, though. "There's not that much to it," he said. "And it's probably already over."

She paced some more. Sipped some more. Though the house had been tightly sealed for days, the scent of the sea had permeated it. The air felt damp and dense enough to clutch by the handful. The thermostat clicked and the air conditioner hummed to life. "Staying here tonight?"

He said, "I don't think so. If what I'm working on isn't really over, it might not be a good idea for me to be around."

She sort of sneered. "Always there's fucking danger in your job. So melodramatic." She was close to losing it. He didn't want to do battle tonight.

"There are melodramatic actors out there who play for real with guns and matches."

Her shoulders sagged. She wasn't up to a fight, either.

Not at the moment, anyway. Good. "Yeah, I guess there are. Real estate's a saner business."

"For saner people."

"Or people crazy in a different way." She finished her drink and began carrying the empty glass toward the kitchen. Such an elegant walk, even in jeans and sandals. He marveled at it. Is that why he was drawn to her? He was a cripple and she covered ground like a dancer?

"Wanna keep me company while I wolf down a micro-waved dinner?" she asked.

He said, "Let's drive someplace. I'll keep you company while you eat real food."

She let out a long breath, finally relaxing, even if not completely. She smiled and said, "Okay, that's a much better idea."

Truce.

Temporarily.

7

CARVER WOKE the next morning to the sounds of the sea, and of Edwina breathing beside him. It was like one sound. The sun had barely risen and the breeze pushing in through the open window was cool on his bare leg sticking out from beneath the thin white sheet. Edwina had worked her way completely out from beneath the sheet and was sprawled on her back with one arm slung loosely across her eyes, as if shielding them from the sun. The air conditioner hadn't kicked in yet, and other than the rhythmic rush of ocean and breathing, the only noise in the room was the gentle ticking of the revolving ceiling fan.

Carver's nose and left cheek were mashed into the pillow. He turned his head, which made his neck ache. Carefully, he rolled onto his side. He studied Edwina's nude form touched by the morning light. Picked up the subtle stale scent of last night's sex and felt something move deep in the core of him. She sighed and dropped her arms to her sides, didn't wake up.

He thought about last night, after Edwina's supper and several drinks at the restaurant bar. The rustle of perspiration-soaked sheets and warm flesh. Her moans. The headboard banging out its primal rhythm against the wall. They were still capable of lust, but he knew last night wasn't any kind of resolution other than physical.

They could continue to rut even as their hearts drifted further apart—if they so chose. And sooner or later neither of them would choose that kind of sex, the kind that meant nothing more than temporary satisfaction; the train to nowhere.

Carver stretched his arm and groped around on the carpet until he found his cane half under the bed. He used it to help him sit up on the edge of the mattress. The singing of the bedsprings didn't affect Edwina. She was sleeping deeply.

He limped into the bathroom and started the shower, adjusting the taps until the water was lukewarm. After leaning his cane against the tile wall, he held on to the towel rack and stepped beneath the stinging needles of spray. Thinking how nice it would be if the water roaring through the pipes and washing so forcefully over his body could cleanse inside as well as out, dissolve the past and afford second chances.

By the time he'd toweled dry and limped nude back into the cool bedroom, Edwina was awake.

Still on her back, she'd pulled the sheet up to cover her nakedness. There was nothing coy about it, he knew; she was simply cool in the morning breeze. She'd fluffed both pillows behind her head and was staring at Carver. Her dark hair was wildly tangled, making her look like a refined savage. Which she could be.

He awkwardly pulled on the Jockey shorts he'd gotten from his stash of clothes remaining at her house, switching hands to lean on his cane. Mr. Nimble.

Watching him through narrowed eyes, as if there were cigarette smoke bothering her, she said, "Leaving?"

"Yeah. I better get to the office in case somebody's been phoning."

"I thought you said the case you were on was ended."

He snapped the shorts' elastic waistband, then glanced around for the rest of his clothes. "All but the murder investigation."

"Whose murder?"

"Woman named Belinda Jackson. Sister-in-law of my client. I mean, former client."

"Killed here in Del Moray?"

"No. In Orlando."

"Desoto's territory."

"Yeah." He sat on the edge of the bed and struggled into his pants. He'd laid them folded on the chair, not carefully enough, because they were very wrinkled. Well, he'd been in a hurry. Barefoot, he limped to the small dresser and got out a fresh pair of socks, then went back to the bed and worked them on. He slipped his feet into the moccasins he didn't have to bother tying. Shoelaces weren't much trouble in the mornings, but he hated it when laces came untied in public, and he had to find someplace to sit down and contort his body simply to tie his shoe. The pitying stares made him furious.

He got a clean brown pullover shirt from the closet and yanked it over his head, then stood at the foot of the bed and tucked it into his pants. Smoothing the thick and curly fringe of gray hair around his ears and at the back of his neck, he caught his reflection in the full-length mirror. Dark pants, dark shirt, catlike blue eyes, harsh features with a scar at the right corner of his mouth that lent him a sardonic expression unless he smiled. Left earlobe missing as the result of a knife wound. He looked like a Paris hoodlum, as usual. Didn't give a fuck, as usual.

Edwina sat up straighter and raked her red-enameled fingernails through her wild hair. It didn't change anything. "Got time to hang around for breakfast?"

"Better not," he said. "Sorry."

"Sure. Well, I gotta get to work anyway. Some choice beachfront property to show."

"Fat commission?"

"If I sell it."

"You will."

She nodded almost solemnly. "Yeah, sooner or later I will."

He limped around the side of the bed to stand over her, then moved the cane close for leverage, leaned down, and kissed her forehead. Her flesh was damp and cool.

She didn't move or look up. " 'Bye, Fred."

He braced on his cane and got out of there.

                              * * *

ACROSS THE street from Carver's office was the pure white
stucco combination courthouse and jail. In the now-glaring
sunlight it looked edible, an iced pastry. Beyond it
stretched the blue and glittering Atlantic. The view was
the stuff of postcards.

The building that housed Carver's office was cream-
colored stucco, low and not very long and with a red tile
roof. His was the end office. The other two businesses in
the building were an insurance brokerage and a car-rental
agency. Customers for all three enterprises came and went,
but nobody was getting rich here.

Carver parked the Olds in its usual slot on the gravel
lot, closer to Golden World Insurance than to his own
office, because the car would be in the shade sooner there
as the sun moved across Magellan and behind the building's roofline.

He raised the canvas top so the vinyl upholstery wouldn't
melt, then limped over and unlocked the office door.
Pushed into the anteroom.

The sun hadn't really gotten mean yet today, and the air
conditioning had the place comfortably cool. By two
o'clock the office would begin to grow warm. Florida in
June, what could he expect? The state really belonged to
the reptiles and other cold-blooded types.

He picked up the mail that had been dropped through
the slot in the door, shuffled the envelopes, and saw nothing that promised a check. Mostly bills and ads. He'd apparently won a video recorder, if only he'd visit a new
condominium development in Fort Lauderdale. Sure. He
tossed the VCR offer and the rest of the obvious junk mail
in the metal wastebasket near the door, then tucked the
few remaining envelopes between his first and second fingers and limped across the sparsely furnished anteroom
toward the open door to his office. He went inside to sit
down behind his desk and check his phone messages and
the rest of the mail.

Stopped after two steps and stood staring.

Somebody was already seated behind his desk, leaning

back in his chair. Somebody else was standing off to the side, next to the window.

The one behind the desk said, "You look surprised."

Carver said, "Am surprised."

"Huh! Huh! Huh!" It was a jackal-like laugh. "Nothing in life should shock you. Not ever. That's just the kinda world it is, you know?"

Carver knew. He said, "You Robert Ghostly this visit? Or Roberto Gomez?"

8

CARVER SAID, "I thought I locked the door."

Gomez smiled. He was wearing a white suit and a pale blue shirt open at the collar. A thick gold chain glinted among his dark chest hairs. He didn't look like a hard-working salesman now. Gomez wore his hair differently, too, from when he'd visited Carver on the beach. It was combed straight back now, greased down almost flat. The slick hairstyle made him look like a lounge lizard, and it made his dense, dark eyebrows seem even more pasted on and out of synchronization. "We don't pay much attention to locks," he said.

Hell with this. Carver limped over to the desk. The man standing didn't actually move from where he leaned with his back against the wall, but an alertness came over his tall, slender body, like a low-wattage current of electricity. He was in his mid-fifties, with a long, loose-fleshed face and sad blue eyes, wearing a dark blue pinstripe suit with a vest. Though it wasn't warm in the office, sweat was rolling down his flabby, somber face. It didn't seem to bother him. One of the two, probably the big one standing, gave off the rancid odor of the unwashed.

"Want something?" Gomez asked, leaning back and gazing up at Carver. As if it were *his* office.

"My chair," Carver said. He gripped the crook of his

cane hard and took a little weight off the tip, ready to use it as a weapon.

Gomez looked amused, but his dark eyes had the flat, emotionless lack of expression Carver had seen on passionless killers. "You serious, my man?"

"About wanting my chair? Yeah."

Gomez worked his eyebrows. His cheek muscles. As if he were holding back a good loud laugh. "Listen, Carver, I give the word and Hirsh starts breaking your small bones. When I'm in a room, I sit where I fucking want. That clear?"

Carver looked over at Hirsh, who looked bored. Also older than Carver had first thought. Gray hairs sprouted from his nostrils and ears, and the black hair on his head looked dyed.

"I asked if that was clear," Gomez said. He didn't look amused now. His tough-guy act was in full swing.

Carver said, "Get up."

Gomez looked surprised. Zoom, zoom went the eyebrows. "Holy fuck! You raised on John Wayne movies or something? Don't you know who I am? Who you're fucking talking to?"

"There's a line I heard in a lot of movies," Carver said, "that 'Don't you know who I am?' thing."

Gomez glanced over at the silent and sober Hirsh. "You wanna do a job on this guy?"

Hirsh shrugged. "Don't matter to me one way or the other."

Gomez looked back at Carver and said, "He means it. It really don't matter diddlyshit to him if he pulls you apart like a plucked chicken or if he don't. Hirsh is like that. Then we go out and get something to eat. I tell you, his appetite stays the same either way."

"Gonna get up?" Carver asked.

Gomez folded his hands on Carver's desk, then bowed his head as if thinking about Carver's request. Like a key executive considering a supplicant employee's plea for a raise.

Then he looked up. His eyebrows were high on his forehead and in line with each other. He was grinning; this wasn't worth going to war over, and he had some sort of use for Carver, otherwise he wouldn't be here. "So siddown, my man." He got up and moved aside in exaggerated fashion so Carver would have room to pass. "You're a fucking gimp, so I oughta mind my manners, right?"

Carver didn't say anything as he limped to his chair and sat down. It was still warm from Gomez; he didn't like that, but other than that it felt good to be sitting. He set his cane off to the side, propping it against the desk where he could grab it if Hirsh or Gomez made a threatening move. He looked at Gomez, who was standing in front of the desk now with his fists on his hips, still smiling, as if he thought Carver was really a hoot. Hirsh was still staring at Carver with his bloodhound gaze, but there might have been a watery glimmer of amusement in his sad blue eyes.

"So why'd you come and see me?" Carver asked Gomez. It was his office again; he was in charge. Sort of.

Gomez stopped smiling. "My wife's sister got herself killed. You were there."

"She didn't *get herself* killed," Carver said. "Somebody shot her. But, yeah, I was there."

"It go down like the news said? A bullet comes through the window and zaps her?"

"That was it," Carver said. "Sniper with a high-powered rifle."

"You see anything at all?"

"Saw your sister-in-law's head explode. That's about it."

"What was the poor dumb cunt doing in our condo?"

"She didn't say. She'd packed some clothes in a suitcase, probably to take to your wife."

"You didn't talk to her?"

"There wasn't time. Fast bullet."

Gomez walked over toward the window, squinting for a moment into the angled, brilliant sunlight. He shot a look at Hirsh, then came back to stand facing Carver and put on a sincere expression. "Her dying was a mistake. You get what I'm saying?"

"Somebody dies that way, it's always a mistake."

"That ain't what I mean, Carver."

"You figure the killer thought she was your wife."

"Yeah. And that's how it looks, right?"

Carver nodded. It did look that way to him. There were only a few black tenants in Beau Capri, and the two sisters would resemble each other through a telescopic sight, especially in Elizabeth Gomez's living room. The killer had probably been waiting patiently for Beth to come home. Maybe he'd never seen her before and only had a description, then made a mistake most people would have made. Most killers. Carver said, "The police'll wanna talk to you."

"That's okay," Gomez said. "There's no warrants out on me. I'll go in and talk, but when I fucking get around to it."

"Police'll get lucky and find you sitting at a desk down at the station house and talking mean, huh? Just like here?"

"You might be surprised, my man. You got the right legal counsel and you can talk mean even in the cop shop. Fucking constitutional rights up the ass. And I got the right attorney."

"Bet you do. Does he know you're here?"

Gomez winked. "Confidential information, Carver."

"If you came here to find out more than was on the news about Belinda Jackson's death," Carver said, "I can't help you. It was quick and simple. The only good thing about it."

"That ain't the purpose of me being here," Gomez said. "I want you to keep looking for Beth. It's obvious she's in danger, and I want her found before something happens to her."

"The police can find her."

"I don't want the police in on it."

"Why not?"

"Nature of my business and all, it ain't a good idea."

Carver saw his point. But he said, "I'm done with you, Gomez. I'll give you back your retainer."

"I won't take it back."

"Okay. I'll spend it. But that changes nothing."

"Why do you want out, Carver?"

"You come to me with a shitpot fulla lies, hire me under false pretenses, and I wind up standing next to a woman when a high-power slug tears into her."

"Coulda been you instead, huh? That it? You chicken-shit, my man?"

"Believe it."

Gomez's eyebrows did their dance and he flashed sharp white teeth. "I *don't* believe it. I do research before I hire somebody, Carver. You got humongous balls, they tell me; they clank when you walk. That's why I wanted *you* and not some sleazy keyhole-peeper'd piss in his pants first time something serious happened."

"Somebody getting shot in the head, that's serious," Carver said. "Serious enough to discourage *me,* anyway."

Gomez crossed his arms and planted his feet wide. Ultimatum time. "Let's put it this way, Carver: You keep searching for Beth, or Hirsh here'll see they'll be searching for your fucking remains."

Carver looked at Hirsh, who gave him a slow smile and a nod. There was a thick gold watch chain draped across his vest, emphasizing a stomach paunch. Hirsh had about him the air of a rough-hewn thug who'd somehow lived long enough to become half a gentleman.

Gomez said, "People I hire, they don't quit."

"Then I've broken new ground."

"*Under* the fucking ground's where you'll be."

Carver said, "I still quit."

"Stubborn fucker!"

"Sure. Those humongous balls." He closed his hand on the cane, ready to lash and stab with it if Hirsh came away from the wall with malice in mind.

Gomez wriggled and jiggled his eyebrows. He seemed puzzled. "Sure you wanna do this, Carver?"

"It's done."

"Don't make goddamn sense."

"Does to me."

Gomez stared at him. "Tell you, in a way I gotta fuck-ing admire you."

"Just business," Carver said. "I don't work for clients who aren't straight with me."

"Well, maybe I can see that. Business is something I understand."

"I've heard that about you."

"Huh! Huh! Huh!" The annoying nasal laugh again. "I just bet you heard plenty, if you asked the right people."

He kept facing Carver and backed slowly toward the door. "C'mon, Hirsh."

Hirsh straightened up away from where he'd been leaning, then ambled over to stand by the door like a theater usher. He was wearing French cuffs, black in contrast to his white shirt. He had incredibly long arms. Huge, gnarled hands with thick, splayed fingers, like sausages flattened at the ends.

"So you think about it," Gomez said, fading toward the anteroom while Hirsh watched Carver and everything else in the office.

"Nothing to think about," Carver said. "It's done. I already quit, sure as Nixon."

"Think about it," Gomez said again. "There's a guaranteed twenty thousand dollars in it for you if you keep looking for Beth, whether you find her or not." He edged past Hirsh and started to cross the anteroom. Hirsh smiled sadly at Carver and followed.

After they'd gone, Carver stayed sitting behind his desk for quite a while, thinking about Gomez's offer, and what Gomez's guarantee was worth.

He decided he really had quit, and he had every reason to stay quit. Nothing about the case called to him.

"Fred Carver?" said a voice from the anteroom.

| 9 |

CARVER STOOD up and limped over to the office door. A short, stocky man stood military-erect in the anteroom, holding a white snap-brimmed straw hat in both hands. He was wearing a neat brown suit, brown shoes, white shirt with a dark brown tie. His visage was stern, his jaw was firm, and he wore his brown hair in a bristle cut. There was an indentation around his head where his hat had pressed. When he saw Carver he said again, "Fred Carver?"

"Me."

"I'm agent Dan Strait, Drug Enforcement Administration."

"I know."

"How?"

"You have the look."

Strait smiled. He still looked stern. "It's a handicap sometimes. I just walk into a place and toilets flush."

"Well, I'm clean," Carver said. "You can search the office for illegal substances."

For a moment Strait seemed to consider the offer. Then he said, "I need to talk to you about the Belinda Jackson murder."

Carver said he'd figured that. He invited Strait into the

office and stood aside to let him pass. Strait walked as if he were leading a parade that was behind schedule.

Carver sat back down behind his desk. Strait flashed his official ID, just as a matter of form, then took the small black vinyl chair. He unbuttoned his brown suit coat and crossed his legs, laid his hat in his lap. "I read the police report on the case. You were in the condo when Miss Jackson was shot, right?"

Carver said that was right. A truck rumbled past outside on Magellan, shifting gears and sending mild vibrations through the office. Carver imagined he could smell exhaust fumes.

Strait said, "Why?"

"Why what?"

"Why were you in the condo?"

"The owner hired me to find his wife. She disappeared from home, so that's where I thought I'd start looking."

"Ah, yes. And your client is—"

"Was," Carver interrupted. "He was in here ten minutes ago and I told him I was off the case."

Strait looked surprised. He tapped the stiff brim of his hat with the fingertips of both hands. "Roberto Gomez was here ten minutes ago?"

"Why? You looking for him?"

"We want to talk to him about the death of his sister-in-law. And we usually know where he is."

"Now you know where he *was*. Along with a guy he called Hirsh."

"And you gave him back his money and bowed out of the missing-wife case, huh?"

"He wouldn't take his money, but I bowed out anyway."

Strait smiled. "Sounds like Gomez; money means nothing and everything to him."

Carver said, "That's not unique. This Gomez as bad as they say?"

"I don't know what they say, but he's as bad as they come. Drug money does that to people."

"What about Hirsh?"

Strait kept his legs crossed. He stopped tapping the hat-brim and crossed his arms. "Hirsh has a record as an enforcer in New Jersey. That's where he hooked up with Gomez, who's from Brooklyn and was a punk criminal in the Northeast before he got into drugs and went south and into the big time. Hirsh is in his sixties, but he's still rough as a cob and not to be fucked with. He does most of Gomez's heavy work. And that's all it is to Hirsh, a job of work. Gomez is a sadistic bastard and gets his jollies watching, but Hirsh might as well be shooting a paper target as a human being. He's a strange man. He brings a kind of dignity to being a killer for pay, but he's still nothing but exactly that: a hired thug."

Carver said, "How big-time is Gomez?"

"He's one of the major players. Maybe the biggest in Florida. He's kept his upper East Coast connections and is able to funnel a lot of narcotics from South America into the New York area. And he's cunning enough to keep changing pickup and drop-off points, and even methods of transport. We've been trying to nail his ass for the past three years and we still haven't got enough to indict. Part of the reason is his ruthlessness; a hotshot like Gomez, we have to work our way up the ladder to build a case. And he doesn't hesitate to saw off the rungs beneath him. Our agents cultivate informers, and Gomez somehow suspects who they are and they simply disappear."

Carver wasn't interested in the details of Gomez's operation. Drug dealers were more common than Amway dealers in Florida. He said, "So who do you think's after his wife? And why?"

Strait gnawed his lower lip, no doubt mulling over whether he should talk freely with Carver. It was he who'd come to Carver's office, apparently to gain Carver's cooperation.

He finally decided as Carver thought he would. He said, "Well, it might be a rival drug faction, wants to kill her out of vengeance for something Gomez did. He gives plenty of people plenty of reason, and it's no secret he's possessive about his wife."

"Maybe she doesn't feel the same way about hubby.

Maybe she's had enough of Gomez and simply skipped out on him.''

"Possibly. But it's more likely she found out somebody's trying to kill her and she's on the run.''

"She figures Gomez can't give her enough protection?''

"Could be. Or maybe it is Gomez she's running from. Maybe it's him trying to kill her and he hired you to find her so he could get to her.''

"I thought you said he loved her.''

"I said he was possessive about her. Anyway, love can flip to hate quick as you can turn an ankle.''

"She doesn't look easy to hate,'' Carver said, "but then I never met her.''

"She's class and he's scum,'' Strait said. "That's what makes their marriage work. I've seen it before. You know how it goes, she's Gomez's prize possession and his chief reward. He's a sleazebag who fought his way to the bottom, and a woman like that allows him to think he's on top.''

"How long they been together?''

"Only a few years. Elizabeth grew up in the slums of Chicago. Got the looks to travel with the rich and famous and found her way to Miami. That's where she met Gomez. And after the embezzler con man she was living with went to prison, she and Gomez became thick.''

"Embezzler still in prison?''

"He was knifed to death there a year ago.''

"Maybe Elizabeth thinks Gomez is responsible.''

"Maybe she does, and probably he *is* responsible. Gomez has influence on both sides of the wall. But a woman like that, it'd make little difference to her. It wouldn't be the reason she might leave Gomez. She might even feel flattered he had somebody killed for her.''

"That how she is?''

"Must be. Or she wouldn't have married Gomez.''

Carver thought that made sense, but he wished he'd found Elizabeth Gomez so he could know why she'd disappeared. If she was still alive. Maybe whoever had killed her sister had rectified the mistake and caught up with Elizabeth by now.

"What else do *you* know about Gomez?" Strait asked.

"Only what you read in the police report. He came to my place up the coast. Said his name was Bob Ghostly and he wanted someone to search for his missing wife. He passed himself off as a medical supply salesman."

"He was one, for six months in New York. But that was ten years ago, when he was between scams. The company fired him for beating up one of the secretaries."

"Charges filed?"

"No. There was no way for her to prove who'd done a job on her, but everyone knew. A few months after Gomez was gone, she was killed by a hit-and-run driver."

"Hirsh?"

"This was before he knew Hirsh. Not Hirsh's style, either. He looks people in the eye when he kills them. They say he even gives the religious a chance to make their peace."

"What a guy," Carver said.

"Well, compared to Gomez he's a saint." Strait stood up and gave Carver a stern look. "Sure you're off this case, Carver?"

"As off it as I can be. I don't work for people like Gomez."

"That's what Lieutenant Desoto said about you. You've got the reputation of a tough guy who's as honest as possible in your line of work, otherwise this interview would have been conducted in another place and another manner. Different questions altogether."

Carver said, "Different answers, too." Wondering what was this hard-ass bureaucrat doing threatening him. But then, some DEA agents were like that. The last one he'd met had been a closet fanatic bent on revenge for a long-ago lynching.

Strait stared at him as if doing some reassessment. He pulled a long black wallet out of an inside pocket, withdrew a card, and laid it on Carver's desk. "Gomez contacts you again, call that number and let me know immediately.''

Carver didn't say he wouldn't, didn't say he would.

Didn't even say good-bye when Strait walked from the office.

| 10 |

AFTER STRAIT had left the office, Carver talked by phone to a Del Moray woman who wanted him to follow her husband to confirm adultery with her teenage sister. She told him she'd be in to see him and make arrangements, but he wasn't sure if she'd show. There was no telling where an investigation might lead, and who'd be hurt by spilled acid. So that kind of thing usually stayed within a family. Sometimes everything worked out, sometimes it festered and the poison spread.

Carver spent most of the day dunning people who owed him money, the only paperwork he enjoyed.

The hours slipped past and the woman who suspected her husband and sister of having an affair didn't come into the office. Carver skipped lunch and ate supper alone in Del Moray, and considered driving by Edwina's to see if she was home. Then he decided against it. He lowered the Olds's canvas top and drove north along the coast toward his beach cottage, while the sea went from blue to dark green as the sun arced like a slow-motion meteor toward land.

SHE WAS waiting inside the cottage, sitting on the small sofa with her legs crossed, wearing a flowered, silky white blouse and white shorts that showed off her tanned thighs.

Seeing her there made Carver ache when he thought of losing her. The dependency he'd feared had become fact.

When he leaned on his cane and closed the door behind him, she said, "I thought we oughta talk."

Carver limped over behind the breakfast counter and opened the refrigerator. He got out a Budweiser and popped the tab, spilling some of the cold, fizzy beer to form a small puddle on the wood floor. Bracing with the cane, he spread the dampness around with the sole of his shoe. He came out from behind the counter and said, "Well, we didn't do much talking last night."

She smiled, remembering. The sun was in the final, rapid stages of setting, softening the light in the cottage and taking ten years off her. Then her face set in hard lines. "I had a conversation with Lester today."

Jack Lester was the real-estate developer who was building the huge condo project in Hawaii and wanted Edwina as marketing director. Carver could imagine what the conversation had been about. He was right.

"I have to let him know within a week whether I'll take the job."

"Pressure," Carver said.

"Lester's under pressure himself."

Carver didn't care about Lester. He took a pull of beer and wiped his mouth with the back of his hand. A gull screamed outside, wheeling in the darkening sky. He said, "You want the job." Not a question.

"Yes," she said.

He stood for a while, leaning on his cane and listening to the ocean whisper ancient secrets. "Gonna take it?"

"I don't know."

He thought she did know.

"Think I should take it?" she asked.

"I don't know." But he did know. Jesus, how did they get into this?

He walked to the wide window and gazed out at the timeless ocean undulating with an orange tint from the sunset behind the cottage. The horizon seemed higher than where he was standing; the sea was overwhelming.

"Fred?"

He turned around to face her. She'd uncrossed her long tan legs and had her knees pressed together, her hands folded in her lap. He said, ''You think love's always a trap?''

She gave him a brief, hopeless smile. ''Maybe that's the nature of the beast; we should ride it while we can before it turns on us.''

''That seems more applicable to wild horses.'' He crushed the empty beer can and tossed it at the wastebasket. Missed. The can clattered on the floor. He'd pick it up later, in the morning.

He limped over to Edwina and leaned down and kissed her lips. She was quietly crying. Not like her to cry.

She sighed and stood up. ''C'mon, Fred.'' She leaned on him as they made their way to the bed.

He made love to her with a passion that knew its time was limited. Used his hands, his mouth. Lost himself in her soft warm flesh while the ocean rushed and ebbed outside.

Afterward, he lay back silently while she slept. He stared out at the darkness and knew that it inevitably consumed love and life and there were no exceptions. Delusions kept people alive, and they were perishable.

But hadn't he always known that? Carver the cynic?

The hot black night enveloped him, and he tried without luck to sleep.

THE NEXT morning he woke up alone and miserable. Edwina had left a note on her pillow saying she needed to get back to Del Moray early for a sales meeting. The sun, glaring like a malevolent orange eye, sent slanted morning light crashing through the wide window to wash the cottage in heat and brilliance.

Carver crumpled up the note and dropped it back on the pillow. Clenching his eyes shut against the aggressive sun, he ran his tongue around the inside of his mouth and grimaced at the terrible taste. He used his cane to help him stand up and hobble to the bathroom, where he immediately brushed his teeth.

He took a hot shower that he gradually adjusted to ice

cold, then toweled himself dry and was feeling somewhat human again as he got dressed. Up to the Paleolithic era, anyway.

Carver limped to the breakfast counter and the Braun coffee-maker Edwina had given him as a birthday present. He rooted in a drawer and saw that there were no filters, just an empty cardboard box. Not that it mattered; there was no coffee, either. Twisting his torso, he reached for the refrigerator door and swung it open. He was looking at three cans of beer, some inedible cottage cheese, a glass decanter with a dribble of orange juice in it. There was some month-old bacon in the meat keeper, he was pretty sure. He closed the door. The refrigerator began to hum, doing what it could to keep things fresh and compensate for his irregular eating habits. GE trying to save him from food poisoning.

He drove to a restaurant on the main highway and had a breakfast of pancakes and sausage, drank three cups of coffee. Carver decided against smoking a cigar, though he felt like it. The Surgeon General and countless cancer studies were hard to shake off. He left a generous tip for the flawlessly efficient and friendly Hispanic waitress, then paid the cashier and limped back out onto the parking lot.

Heat radiated up through the thin leather soles of his moccasins. It was only ten o'clock and the temperature was already in the nineties.

He brushed away a large mosquito that wanted blood from one of his nostrils, then limped toward the Olds. The mosquito followed; he heard it drone past his right ear, felt it light on the back of his neck. He slapped at it and heard it buzz away. It seemed discouraged, anyway.

As soon as he got the Olds's engine running, he put the top up and switched the air conditioner on high.

Then he got back on the highway and stopped at the B&B Fast Food Market just as the car's interior was beginning to cool down. He needed coffee and more beer.

As he was picking up a can of Folger's coffee, he noticed a woman staring at him from the other end of the aisle, near a display of pickles that were on sale. She was black and had on an oversized cheap gray dress. Flat white shoes like the ones nurses wore. Amber-tinted sunglasses. There was a wide-brimmed white canvas hat pulled low on her head, the kind a lot of boaters in the area wore, that concealed most of her hair. He thought she was about fifty.

But when she left the sweet dills and came toward him, the tall body beneath the baggy dress moved with the fluidity of youth. She was younger than fifty, or she wore her age with impressive grace.

A few feet from him, she pretended to study brands of tea. Then she turned to him, floated up a hand, and lowered the tinted lenses to focus her gaze on him. She had long, pointed fingernails, he noticed, unpainted, and beautiful brown eyes that tilted slightly up at the corners and gave her a vaguely Oriental look.

He knew who she was and didn't want this to be happening, didn't know how to figure it.

She said, ''Fred Carver?''

''He's my brother.''

She didn't smile. In fact, she looked gravely serious. ''I'm Elizabeth Gomez. Bet you can't guess what I want.''

She had him there.

11

ELIZABETH GOMEZ stood by the tea and said, "All I want's about ten minutes of your time."

Carver shook his head no. "Sorry. I want nothing to do with you or your husband, Mrs. Gomez. You'll have to work out your own problems."

She had the tinted glasses up on the bridge of her nose again; he couldn't see her eyes. "Our problems are beyond working out, Carver. The relationship has ended."

Carver couldn't help it; he decided to go fishing. "Roberto still cares for you enough to hire someone to find you and bring you back."

"We both know why he wants me found," she said in a soft, level voice. "He wants me dead, and locating me's the first step. You didn't know it at the time, Carver, but he hired you to be the finger man."

"Finger man?"

"The one who points out the victim so the hit man can do his job. And if you're still around and in the way, like at the condo when my sister was shot by mistake, you get a bullet yourself. You hadn't got out of the line of fire there, you'd have been found dead lying next to Belinda." She peeked at him over the plastic frames of the glasses again. "Know how the hit man can get right to his job once the target's been found? He follows the finger man,

65

especially if the finger man don't know shit about why he's looking for somebody. That way there's no time wasted, no opportunity for the target to slip away. Ever since my husband hired you, he's had somebody shadowing you.''

Carver thought she was probably telling the truth. It made him uneasy, and more than a little angry. "I take it since I quit the case, I'm no longer being watched."

"Take it however you like, Carver. Nobody knows what the fuck a man like my husband's gonna do. That's part of the secret of his success. And part of the reason I left him.''

An elderly woman with dyed red hair pushed a shopping cart up the aisle, glared at them as she had to detour around Elizabeth Gomez, who didn't budge an inch to get out of the way. When the woman had huffily grabbed a can of coffee, then made her way to the pickle display at the end of the aisle, Elizabeth said, "This is no place for what I need to say."

"We got nothing to talk about."

"I say we do." She smiled. "Anyway, I'm not leaving you any choice. I'll stick close to you as Superglue till you let me have my say, and if my husband's hired men find me and follow orders, you'll go along on the dark ride with me.''

"Dark ride," Carver said. "I like that. It's poetic."

"Let's rap, then. I'll entertain you some more."

Carver thought about it. Thought about it for a while. "You got a car outside?"

"Uh-hm. Didn't walk."

"Let me pick up a few more groceries. Then, when I drive away, follow me to my place. It's not far from here."

She said, "I know where it is."

Carver set the cane's tip and limped away from her, over to the cooler, where he pulled out a couple of cold Budweiser six-packs. He couldn't ward off the thought that if he let Gomez know he had his wife at the cottage, she'd be worth twenty thousand dollars. Not that he'd consider doing it. And Elizabeth Gomez was right, he'd never see the twenty thousand; Gomez would snip all loose ends to her murder, one of which would be Carver.

He gathered up a quart of milk and a dozen large eggs. Some vitamin-fortified cornflakes with TV cartoon characters on the box. He carefully selected a head of lettuce that would probably turn brown in his refrigerator. On the way to the front of the store, he found room between the groceries tucked beneath his arms to fit in a can of sliced peaches. For the cornflakes.

Impulse buyer, he admonished himself. He shouldn't have reached for the peaches. And he shouldn't have listened even as long as he had to Elizabeth Gomez. There was a point where judgment crumbled.

He checked out in the express lane, behind a guy not only with more than ten items, but with half a cart full of groceries. That was criminal, but the checkout girl let him get away with it, so what could Carver do?

Still irked by having to wait in line, he carried his paper sack of groceries to his car. He didn't look around as he set the sack on the front seat, slid it over, then leaned on his cane and lowered himself in behind the steering wheel.

He drove from the parking lot onto the main highway and headed toward the turnoff to his cottage. A steady breeze was bearing in from the east, bringing with it the rot-and-life scent of the sea. Death and renewal. Had the ocean smelled the same a million years ago?

A small white car, a Ford Escort, appeared in the corner of his rearview mirror and stuck there like a decal. Elizabeth Gomez was driving, still wearing her tinted glasses.

AT THE cottage, Carver sat in a webbed aluminum chair with his stiff leg propped up on the porch rail. Elizabeth Gomez refused his offer of the other chair and stood leaning with her buttocks against the rail, her back to the glittering sea. They were in the deep shade of the porch roof, sipping Budweiser from the can. She'd parked the Escort, which Carver noticed had a rental company bumper sticker, alongside the cottage, almost out of sight.

The first thing she said was, "You're no longer being followed, but Roberto still thinks you might accept his twenty-thousand-dollar offer. That you'll find me and give me to him.''

Carver touched the base of the moisture-beaded can to his thigh. Cold condensation worked through the material of his pants. ''How do you know all that?''

''I have a few friends in my husband's organization. If I ask, they take a chance, tell me things I should know. They told me Roberto hired you under false colors. You accepted the job, then you backed off when you found out what was going on.'' She took a sip of beer and placed the can on the rail. She'd removed the tinted glasses, and it looked for a moment as if her dark eyes were misting. ''After Belinda got killed.''

''If you know I know the story,'' Carver said, ''what do we have to talk about?''

She removed the wide-brimmed hat now. Her hair, raven black and straightened, tumbled to her shoulders, changing her appearance entirely. Made her look like a rock singer, or a funky fashion model. Even the baggy gray dress couldn't hide the lissome curves of her lean body. He'd heard Elizabeth was a beautiful woman. Heard right. She said, ''You don't know the whole story.''

''About your pregnancy?''

''Yeah.''

''And why you left your husband?''

''Yeah again.''

''I don't care,'' Carver said. ''Domestic difficulties don't interest me. They're not my business. Point is, you want out, Gomez doesn't want you out, and he's a tough guy to leave.''

''Oh, he's not that hard to leave. Only thing is, you leave everything else when you leave Roberto. I mean, like life itself.''

Carver gazed beyond the toe of his moccasin, at the ocean rolling in the sunlight. A pelican flapped past, dipped suddenly at a fish. Made a splash but came up empty and flapped on. ''Here's how it is,'' Carver said. ''I believe he's trying to kill you, and I think you oughta go to the police. Trade what you know in exchange for their protection.''

She shook her head, staring at him with those dark, dark eyes. "Can't do that."

"Why not?"

"Roberto's into drugs in a big way."

"Not news to many."

"I'm into drugs too."

"I told you, work a deal. Get immunity. The law wants to put Roberto away, Elizabeth."

"Do me a favor and call me Beth. I don't like formality."

"Okay, Beth."

"What you want me to call you?"

"Carver's fine."

"I don't mean I'm into drugs that way. Carver, the way Roberto is." She was staring fixedly at him, something in her eyes pleading for understanding. "Not as a dealer."

He tapped gently on the porch rail with his cane. Not making much noise. "You telling me you're a user?"

"That's it. Couldn't just say no, I'm afraid."

"Heavy user?"

"The heaviest. And that's no exaggeration."

Carver said, "What's that change?"

"Roberto doesn't do drugs," she said. "Nobody who works for him does. He figures that's the only way to run his business. It's a strict rule. Strict rule for me not to use any of the stuff, either."

"But you broke the rule."

"Been breaking it for the past two years. Did coke at first. Then heroin."

"Heroin, huh." Almost disinterested. Then he said, "Oh, Jesus!"

She had a way of knowing what he was thinking. "That's right. Our baby—Roberto's son—died from addiction complications immediately after birth. That's why Roberto wants to kill me, even though he knows my own addiction's such it'll probably kill me within a year or so."

It was difficult for Carver to feel sympathy for her. A baby born with the raging blood of her habit, too frail to survive, where was there room for compassion for the mother? For an instant he knew how Gomez must feel.

Why he needed vengeance. "How's Roberto know you're hooked that badly?"

"The doctor told him. The one that delivered the baby. Roberto wanted as few people as possible to know I was pregnant. That's why he put me in the condo in Orlando. He arranged for me to have the baby at a private clinic, run by a doctor he knows. The doctor told him what happened, and I found out Roberto was furious. The day after the birth, I got out of the clinic. I laid low at a friend's place till I healed up enough to get on the run, and I been running ever since." She swallowed, her Adam's apple working in her lean brown throat. "Roberto wants his revenge. That's the way he is. He wants me before Mr. Heroin can have me."

Carver looked out at the hazy horizon. She had to be in the last and worst stages of her habit to have killed her child. She was being optimistic in saying she had a year or two at most to live. A heroin addict in her league could measure the future in months. He said, "Does it really matter much which way you go, or how soon?"

She looked hard at him, and it seemed for a moment as if she might break down and sob. "Get yourself in my position, you hard-ass bastard. Find out how it feels. See how much you love life."

"Maybe you're right. But I'll ask you what I asked Roberto the day he showed up here to hire me. Why me?"

"Because you got the courage to turn down Roberto. You refused to help him murder me, even for twenty thousand. Know what that means?" She was quietly sobbing now. Her body was quaking inside the baggy gray dress. The body he'd assumed was lean and sensuous was a doper's wracked, thin frame, shaking itself in despair.

"Means I got humongous balls?"

"Damn you!" She turned away, toward the sea, so he couldn't see her crying.

He sat sipping beer, not liking himself. Telling himself he didn't feel compassion for her, this woman who'd chosen a fast life and then killed her child with her weakness. Carver couldn't help it; weakness had always repelled him. In himself, especially, but too often in others who'd had some choice in the matter. What was free will about, if not that?

She turned around to face him again, composed now. "Everybody's got some kinda weakness," she said. She was a goddam psychic.

He said, "I wouldn't argue it."

She stood up straight. She was probably about five-ten. "You gonna help me, Carver?"

He said, "I'm sorry, I don't do bodyguard work."

Her demeanor changed. She moved closer to where he sat. Gazed down at him as if *she* pitied *him*.

Then she nodded. He wasn't worth speaking to. She'd made her appeal and failed, and that was that.

She walked from the porch toward her car, not glancing back at him, her head held high. There was something unmistakably defiant in her long, loose-jointed stride. Even haughty. He'd doomed her and she was saying piss on him, she didn't need him after all in order to die the way she wanted.

He liked that about her, that spit-in-the-eye quality. Liked it a lot. But he didn't try to stop her as she drove away.

| 12 |

WHEN CARVER drove to his office and turned off of Magellan, he saw a black Lincoln stretch limousine in his usual parking slot near Golden World Insurance. It had darkly tinted windows and several different kinds of little antennae sticking up from its trunk. An occupant could coast along unseen and listen in on broadcasts from Mars.

He parked next to the Lincoln and took care not to bump its gleaming and reflective side as he opened the Old's heavy, rusty door.

As he raised himself up out of the car, he heard a steady, ticking whisper and realized the limo's motor was idling. Heat was rolling out from beneath it. The rear window on Carver's side glided down and Gomez smiled out at him.

"C'mon into *my* office and talk this time," Gomez said. "Cooler than yours."

Carver hesitated, then figured what the hell. He limped around the smoothly idling Lincoln and opened the passenger-side rear door. Leaned down and looked inside before getting in.

The car was equipped with a well-stocked miniature bar and a color TV that was soundlessly playing a soap opera. On the other side of a glass partition sat the driver, facing straight ahead. His shoulders were slightly stooped. His thinning black hair was parted and combed sharply to the side, and tufts of gray hair sprouted from his long ears. Had to be Hirsh. He was the only occupant of the car other than Gomez and glitz.

Gomez said, "You're letting the cool air out, Carver."

Carver used his cane for balance and slid in to sit next to Gomez on soft leather upholstery. He pulled the foot-thick door shut and was in another world of coolness and quiet. There was no sound inside the spacious limo other than the gentle whir of an air conditioner blower, no engine vibration.

Gomez scooted around so he was half-facing Carver across the wide seat. He fixed his black button eyes on Carver and worked his out-of-sync eyebrows as if to let Carver know he was amused. "So, you been thinking about my offer?"

"Nothing to think about," Carver said. "I already refused it."

Gomez surprised him. "Okay. I wouldn't wanna force somebody to work for me if he didn't wanna give it his fucking all, you know?"

"Makes sense. Hundred and ten percent and all that."

"Right. So what I came to tell you is we're doing a one-eighty-degree turn here, my man. What I'm saying is stay as clear of me and mine as you can get. I don't wanna see or hear of you again. Our business is finished, like you want it to be."

Carver wondered if Gomez had somehow learned about Beth talking to him. It didn't seem possible. Couldn't have anything to do with why Gomez was here.

Unless Beth had been followed from the cottage and killed, and now Gomez was warning Carver not to tell the law about her visit or the subject of their conversation.

Carver's mouth was dry. He said, "Why the change of direction?"

Gomez grinned. Oh, those eyebrows. "It ain't for you to worry about."

"Maybe you already found your missing wife."

"Maybe. Who knows."

Carver couldn't let it lie. He had to probe. He had no compassion for Beth Gomez, but he didn't like the idea of this dope-rich Napoleon dropping by now and then to control his life. Too much money and power. Too much arrogance. He said, "I know about what happened to your son."

Gomez's face darkened and a tremor shook his body beneath his expensive gray suit. In that instant Carver knew Beth's fears were justified. Gomez wanted her, all right. Probably hadn't found her yet, but wanted her. "How'd you find out about my son?" he asked in a tight voice.

Carver said, "I'm a detective, like my card says."

"Ain't you, though. Well, my man, I guess you know then why I want the cunt back."

"I can imagine."

Gomez smiled all over except for the deathlike button eyes beneath the comic brows. "I bet you can't." He leaned back into the encompassing tufted upholstery. The movement stirred the air and the scent of his after-shave filled the back of the limo. "Listen, I save this girl from the fucking sewer. Treat her like a goddam queen. Even used to call her Queen Elizabeth, can you believe it? She turns up pregnant 'cause she forgets to take a pill, but I'm a nice guy about it. I don't push her into an abortion. So she stays knocked up. I don't care, if she wants it so bad. Even get used to the idea. Could be a son, another *me*, you know? So I get real fond of the fatherhood role I see coming at me. I make sure she gets the best of medical attention." He abruptly slapped the seat, startling Carver. The noise reached the front of the car, and Hirsh's head snapped around. Hirsh saw everything was okay. Glanced at Carver through the glass as if he were viewing sea life in an aquarium, then turned back to gaze out over the steering wheel at Golden World Insurance.

Gomez said, "All I do for the bitch, and what do I find out? She's been dipping into the stock. Got herself a habit. She's a fucking heroin user, already halfway to hell. You know the average life of somebody's been on that stuff super-heavy, Carver?"

"Couple of years?"

"At best. I mean, I sell it, so I oughta know. But I tell you, I never suspected. She's built real lean anyway, so there wasn't any weight loss to tip me off. And she's smart. Took mail-order college courses, all that shit. Probably what fucked her up. But she knew how to trick me into thinking she was clean; I give her that. Fooled me until the doctor came and told me about how her addiction killed my baby son. How the heroin in the mother's blood found its way into the womb and the baby's own blood. I didn't know the news'd hit me so hard, not till I heard it.'' He was trembling, either from pity or rage. "A tiny body like that, Carver, it can't handle that shit. That's what the doctor told me. He didn't say it in those words, but any way you say it, my son died less than an hour after he was born.''

"What'd Beth say when you saw her?''

"I never did see her after I heard. When I got to the medical clinic, she was smart enough to have cleared the hell out. I been looking for her ever since, and I'll fucking keep looking.''

Carver didn't doubt it.

Gomez was sitting stiffly, powerful jaw muscles flexing like living beings beneath his skin as he clenched his teeth. A vein in his neck was throbbing, a blue hammer pounding out time.

"If her habit's gonna kill her soon enough anyway,'' Carver said, "why should you bother looking for her?''

Gomez gave a kind of snorting laugh, as if Carver's question was so stupid it didn't warrant an answer.

Maybe Gomez was right. When Carver's son died, he'd felt the same way.

Gomez's chest heaved. A stillness came over his body. He was himself again, the emotionless, tough entrepreneur in the toughest of businesses. "You ain't in, so you're out, Carver. All the way out. That's what I want you to understand. I don't want you around complicating things. Because if I figure it'd be less complicated to see that you disappear in the swamp country, then you'll be introduced to some alligators. We clear on that?''

Carver said, "Alligators or crocodiles?''

Gomez didn't blink. "The hard-guy act'll carry you only so far. Till you become food.'' He rapped on the glass partition and Hirsh made a slight movement, reaching for something.

There was a muted click from the door next to Carver. He hadn't realized he was locked in.

Gomez was staring straight ahead. He said, "Good luck, stranger."

Carver worked the door handle. Pushed open the vault-like door and felt hot outside air close in on him. He said, "Wait here a minute, okay?" and didn't move until Gomez had nodded.

Then he limped into his office and over to the file cabinet. He unlocked the fireproof bottom drawer and got out the envelope containing the thousand dollars Gomez had given him as a retainer to find his wife.

When he returned to stand by the back of the limo, Gomez lowered the power window. The soap-opera volume was up now on the TV; a woman said, "God, I love you, Damien. I'll love you forever!" Carver had never known anyone named Damien. He handed Gomez the envelope, then watched him lift the flap and look inside. Money was obviously his intimate friend.

Gomez frowned. He didn't understand this and didn't like it. "Why you giving this back?"

Carver said, "I didn't earn it."

"That don't mean shit to me, Carver."

"Guess it wouldn't."

Gomez stared at him with eyes that seemed to absorb rather than reflect light. He said, "Stay out of my life, you hear?"

Carver said, "I'm glad to be out of it."

The tinted window slid back up and the limo backed out of its parking slot, made a sharp turn to the driveway, then accelerated smoothly out onto Magellan.

Carver stood in the searing sun, watching the long black car until it disappeared, wondering himself why he'd returned the money.

13

THE WOMAN who suspected her husband and sister of having an affair called again and apologized to Carver for not showing up for their appointment. She said she'd had second thoughts; she was afraid of what he might find out. He told her he understood, and that when she got straight in her mind what she wanted to do about the situation, he'd still be available to help her. He didn't think she'd call back.

Only a minute or so after he'd hung up, McGregor walked into the office. If everybody who hated McGregor formed a single-file line, it would be hard to walk around it. Del Moray police lieutenant McGregor was an infuriating man to be around; he saw humanity as rotting meat and himself as a happy maggot. It was difficult to deal with someone like him, who embraced, and even exulted in, being completely amoral. Sometimes his logic was impeccable.

He was a coiled and lanky six and a half feet of bad taste and bad manners. He had on a cheap brown suit that hung from his bony shoulders as if from a bent hanger. His white shirt was wrinkled and stained. The narrow end of his kinked tie dangled below the wide. His huge brown wingtip shoes were scuffed. He loomed in an almost visible odorous cloud of the perfumey cheap cologne he favored over bathing. Grinning his gap-toothed smile, he shoved back the straight lock of his lank blond hair that always flopped over his forehead, stared at Carver with his intense, close-set pale blue eyes. He had a long, narrow face with a prognathous jaw, a ruby of dried blood on his chin where he'd cut himself shaving.

Carver tried not to breathe the cologne-fouled air too deeply and said, "You given up knocking on doors?"

McGregor kept smiling. He propped his giant's hands on his hips. "I like to walk in unexpected on shitballs like you. Catch them off guard so I can see how the lower fifth lives."

"You got an upside-down view of the world," Carver said.

McGregor stuck the tip of his tongue, like a pink viper, through the wide gap between his yellowed front teeth. His grin became more of a leer as he said, "How's you and your lady sackmate getting along these days?"

Carver couldn't help it; he felt the anger stir in him. He put on a calm act, wondering if McGregor had somehow found out about his troubles with Edwina.

"Can't answer, asshole? Tongue-tied by love? Or just tongue-tired?"

"That why you're here, to ask me about my love life?"

"Hardly worth my time to find out how some gimp does it between the sheets." McGregor probed at a molar with his tongue, staring at Carver with his cheek lumped out grotesquely. Then he said, "I see by the news you got yourself mixed up in a murder over in Orlando."

"Not in your jurisdiction," Carver said.

"But *this* is my jurisdiction, fuckface. Where we're looking at one another right now. The name Roberto Gomez was in the same news items. It was his sister-in-law got herself offed, right?"

"Still in Orlando," Carver said, "not Del Moray."

"Well, I'd be remiss in my duties if I learned a known big-time drug lord like Gomez was in my fair city and I didn't find out why. He left your office not long ago, didn't he?"

Carver figured McGregor had put a watch on the office

after hearing about the murder in the Gomez condo. He hoped McGregor hadn't had the smarts or the manpower to watch the beach cottage up the coast, or he'd know about Beth Gomez's visit. "Gomez was here," Carver said. "He was my client for a while. He's not anymore."

"Sure. Assuming I trust you to tell me the truth. But the fact is, I trust you about as far as you can hobble without your cane."

Carver shrugged. "Makes no difference to me what you believe."

"Should, though," McGregor said.

Carver leaned back in his chair and looked up at the long head on top of the basketball center's body. "How come you're interested in this?"

McGregor sneered down at Carver as if that were a stupid question. "I told you, Gomez is a big-time drug dealer and he's here in my city talking to some pissant private eye. Big time means big bucks, hey? *Real* big bucks, since it's drug money."

"And you want some of it?"

"Christ, Carver, I'm a policeman!" Saliva sprayed as McGregor feigned indignation. Some of it speckled Carver's bare forearm. Made him nauseated. McGregor wiped a fleck of dampness from his chin and started his shaving cut bleeding again.

"Some policeman," Carver said, watching the worm of fresh blood ease its way toward the point of McGregor's long chin.

"Let's just say that all the money involved means nailing Roberto Gomez can make a hardworking cop's career."

"If the cop survives."

"Sure. And he will if he's smart. He'll be promoted to captain, most likely."

"Someday even chief."

"I got no desire to be chief."

"I know better."

"So you think. But I'm not surprised you think small, Carver."

"And I'm not surprised you think bigger than you are.

You think you'll bypass the rank of captain and move on to better things? Maybe they'll make you dictator?''

"Something like that. If a person was considering tossing his hat in the ring for the mayoral election next year, it'd be better if it was a captain's hat and not a lieutenant's. You follow?''

"I follow,'' Carver said. "And where it goes is horrific.'' He knew McGregor was capable of fooling enough of the people enough of the time. Capable of anything, actually; he was a man with the brashness of Napoleon and the scruples of Hitler, not to mention a crude Machiavellian deviousness.

"You don't think I'd make a good mayor?''

"I think you'd make a good politician, as long as the voters didn't get to know you. Nobody's better equipped with the necessary ego and moral vacuum.''

"You call it a moral vacuum, I call it pragmatism. I see the world the way it is. You see it through your boxtop code of honor you shoulda grown outa by the third grade. You sent in for your secret decoder ring yet, fuckhead?''

"What made you consider this possible jump into politics?''

"Everything's politics,'' McGregor said. "Politics is just *called* politics. And I have it on pretty good authority that the mayor doesn't plan on running for reelection. Something about a potential scandal.''

"Would you have anything to do with that?''

"I told you, everything's politics.''

Carver toyed with the crook of his cane. "Well, there's no political hay for you to make here. I'm out of anything concerning Roberto Gomez. And I guess you ran a check on him and found out he's not a fugitive.''

"Orlando police'd like to talk with him regarding the death of his sister-in-law,'' McGregor said.

"But he's not a suspect.''

"Guy like that, he's always a suspect. That's why the DEA's on him like flies on shit.''

"So what do I do to get you to leave?'' Carver asked. "You after a political donation?''

"I'll talk to you about that if I become a candidate,''

McGregor said seriously. "Right now I just wanted you to know I'm in the game here. You find out anything pertinent, you let me know or I'll ream your ass."

"Well, since you ask politely . . ."

McGregor flashed his gap-toothed grin again, probing between his front teeth with his tongue. He got his lanky body turned around section by section and moved toward the door, then paused and said, "Say hello to your lady love, hey?"

"Sure. She's always glad to hear from you. Likes it when her skin crawls."

The grin stayed. "Some of 'em do. Incidentally, you get tired of running through that, send it around to see me."

Carver gripped his cane with aching, whitened knuckles. Held it as a jabbing weapon and stood up, leaning on the desk. "You get tired of breathing, step over here closer."

Still smiling, McGregor walked out the door. He was obviously pleased; he'd gotten under Carver's skin again.

Carver sat back down. He was breathing hard. The office seemed smaller and more confining. The dense air still reeked of perfumey cologne.

Carver stood up and limped over to the window. It couldn't be opened, but just looking outside made it seem easier to breathe. He watched the unmarked Pontiac, McGregor's tall form bent over the steering wheel so he'd have headroom, turn onto Magellan and pass from sight.

He knew McGregor had successfully goaded him, and he didn't like it.

Mayor McGregor.

My God, it had a ring to it!

| 14 |

CARVER DROVE to the Del Moray marina for lunch. He sat in a window booth at the Sea Delite restaurant, ate deep-fried shrimp, and sipped cold Budweiser while he thought about McGregor's visit.

Outside of Gomez's circle, only Carver had talked with Beth Gomez and knew that Roberto wasn't trying to find his wife to protect her, but to kill her. Gomez had undoubtedly hired the sniper who'd murdered Beth's sister, and if the law could prove it, Gomez would be charged with homicide if not drug trafficking. The result would be the same with either charge: a future of locks and bars.

Carver dipped a shrimp in cocktail sauce and popped it into his mouth, wondering as he chewed if it had been Hirsh on the roof of the building across from the Gomez condo. Probably not. Gomez had a stable of thugs at his disposal; he'd have stationed men at points where Beth might show up. Men with orders to kill. There was no shortage of people who'd obey that order in the world Gomez lived in, because there was no choice but to obey. Life, and death, made simple.

Carver ordered another beer and watched the smooth white hulls of pleasure boats bob gently in unison at their moorings. Del Moray was for the most part a wealthy retirement community, and some of its well-fixed citizens were playing with their floating toys. The white hair, white belts, and white shoes out there in the sun almost caused the eye to ache. Stomach paunches burdened most of the men. The lean, tanned limbs and torsos of many of the women foretold how they'd not only outlive their over-weight husbands but would look years younger at the funerals. Wealthy, attractive widows with yachts were always in demand. Topmasts and tummy tucks. Florida was the land of the plastic surgeon, as well as beaches, Disney, drugs, and a nasty strain of zealous fundamentalist religion. Still, Carver knew if he went with Edwina to Hawaii, he'd miss it.

He finished his beer, settled with the waitress, then drove back to the office. There was a rental car in the only shady spot on the lot, so Carver parked the Olds in the sun and limped across the baking gravel to shove open the door to his reception room. He'd turned the thermostat down, and cool air hit him like a chilled weave. Felt great.

He'd limped to his desk and was checking his answering machine for messages (none) when the phone rang. Snatching up the receiver before the end of the second ring, when his recorded outgoing message would begin, he identified himself and waited for the caller to speak.

"This is Beth Gomez, Carver."

He thought about hanging up, but instead said, "Hello," rather stupidly.

"I wanna talk to you again." Fear gave her voice a jagged edge, as if her words hurt her throat.

"We already talked."

"There's something I shoulda told you but didn't."

"Tell me now."

"Not on the phone."

"All right, come over to my office."

"I can't. Roberto might have somebody watching it."

"Not since he personally and forcefully accepted my resignation," Carver said.

"Ha! Roberto doesn't accept resignations."

Maybe she had a point; Gomez wasn't accepting hers with good grace, unless you didn't count trying to kill her.

"Meet me in the park near the marina?" she pleaded.

Carver said, "I just came from the marina."

"I know. I saw you there. At first I didn't have a chance to approach you. Then, when I could have walked over to you, I was too afraid. By the time I'd made up my mind, you'd driven away."

"What were you doing at the marina?"

"I followed you there from your office, after that tall man left. If the restaurant hadn't been so crowded I'd have contacted you there, but I couldn't risk it. Crowds make me jumpy these days. He a cop, the tall, mean-looking guy?"

"Sort of. Why?"

"It's kinda stamped on him."

"You must wanna talk to me in the worst way," Carver said.

"It's more important than life or death."

What the hell did that mean?

"I gotta hang up," she said. "Been on the line almost long enough for the call to be traced."

"You on a public phone?"

"Yeah."

"Then don't worry."

"Carver, you just don't know what and who drug money'll buy. I'm not even sure your phone's not tapped. But I've gotta take a chance here. I'll wait for you in the park. On one of the benches facing the ocean."

"I didn't say I was coming."

"I know. But I'll pray you'll turn up. You're the kinda guy who answers prayers."

"Not all of them."

"Didn't say you were a saint." She hung up.

Carver replaced the droning receiver in its cradle. The office that had felt so cool when he'd first walked in now seemed too warm.

He didn't have to meet with Beth Gomez in the marina park, but he knew he would. He wasn't sure why. Maybe because whoever had sent a bullet into Belinda Jackson's head should have to pay. Maybe because Roberto Gomez was a walking danger that belonged in prison. Or maybe because he, Carver, knew down deep the truth of what

Beth Gomez had just mentioned: Roberto wasn't the type to accept resignations. Or possibly Carver was exactly what he'd been told he was, a dog with a rag.

He did know he wasn't meeting Beth Gomez to answer her prayer. He knew himself that well. He wasn't a saint, he was a survivor.

SHE WAS where she said she'd be, seated on one of the pale concrete benches that faced the ocean and its wide horizon.

Carver had made sure he wasn't followed. He parked the Olds near the white Ford Escort she'd driven earlier to his cottage. Then he limped across the hard, uneven ground toward where she sat, careful about where he planted the tip of his cane.

She was just sitting there watching him. She hadn't moved. When he got closer, he saw she had some sort of bundle in her lap. She'd shed the baggy gray dress and wasn't trying to disguise her beauty now, had on khaki safari pants with oversized flap pockets and a thick belt pulled tight around her waist. Her tailored white blouse's collar was spread wide enough to reveal a gold necklace against smooth, dusky flesh. Her breasts hinted at firmness and bulk beneath the blouse. Caused Carver to wonder what she looked like nude. She had straightened hair parted on the side now, neatly combed. A touch of purple eye shadow. Her features seemed more delicate, except for her wide, angular cheekbones. Born into another life, she might have become a rich and famous model. On the other hand, in her own fashion, she'd capitalized plenty on her looks.

When Carver sat down next to her on the hard bench, he saw that the bundle in her lap was a bunched blue blanket.

It squawked.

Beth drew aside a corner of the blanket and a tiny, dazed face scrunched up when the light hit it. She got a bottle from the folds of the blanket, fit the nipple in the infant's mouth, and said, "This is Adam." Her tone suggested

Carver should shake the kid's hand and call him a likely lad.

Carver was trying to put it all together, but none of it fit quite right. "Adam Gomez?"

Beth nodded, gazing down at the infant the way women do, as if posing for a church's stained-glass window. "My son. And Roberto's."

Carver watched the baby work on the rubber nipple, then watched the masts of the moored sailboats doing their swaying, subtle dance in rhythm with the waves that washed gently against the dock. What was going on? What was the deal here? He said, "You told me Gomez was after you because the child had died due to your heroin addiction."

"Well, that wasn't exactly true."

"Then what is?"

As she spoke, she rocked the baby ever so gently. "Let me tell you, Carver, I grew up in a slum in Chicago. Like most ghetto kids, I wanted the fast and expensive life; that's the values you get in a place like that."

"Sure, I understand."

"Doubt it. Anyway, I got outa there the only way I knew how, using what Mother Nature gave me before Father Time took it away."

Carver thought about that, then said, "You're still a few steps ahead of Father Time."

Beth glanced over at him, somehow acknowledging the compliment with only those big, dark eyes. She was used to such remarks and had had practice. "I got mixed up with Roberto and lived the fastest of the fast life. Money, cars, sex, power. Then, a couple of years ago, I was surprised to find myself getting sick of my life. And sickened by what I'd become. Sounds stupid, but I wanted to do some giving instead of taking, even up whatever scales there are. Roberto wouldn't understand. Couldn't. But he let me more or less do what I wanted, and I began associating with people outside his crowd. Even took some correspondence courses from Florida State University."

"You don't sound like you're from the ghetto," Carver noted. "Not much slang and slide in the way you talk."

"I pretty much worked that outa myself long ago, so I'd be acceptable wherever rich men wanted to take me. Though I admit my college communication courses helped some, too. Anyway, when I became pregnant last year I was pleased, but Roberto wasn't. Not at first. I talked him outa forcing me into an abortion, and when he got used to the idea of fatherhood, he became more enthusiastic than I was over having a son. He never even considered it'd be a girl, and he was right. During my months of pregnancy I began to think about raising my child. I really saw what I was. What Roberto was. What kind of life I'd be bringing my baby into. I didn't want it to be that way. I decided it *wouldn't* be that way."

"What about your drug habit?"

"Never actually had one. I secretly put together some money, which wasn't difficult the way we lived. Money flowed all around Roberto, like a river around an island. I bribed the doctor who delivered Adam. He told Roberto the baby died because I was heavily addicted to heroin." She looked away from the child and directly at Carver. "I thought we'd have a chance that way, a door out. Roberto would think his son was dead. He'd think *I'd* be dead within a short time, like most heroin freaks. I could live on what I had for a while, then get some kinda job under another identity and bring Adam up right, not in an environment of narcotics and death and twisted values. Call it the American dream."

Carver held his cane with both hands. Jabbed at the ground a few times with its tip. There she sat with her son; he had to believe this one. It made sense. A woman begins thinking of her child and not just of herself, and she wants out of the kind of life Beth Gomez had been living. Wants the child's father to stay out of the picture. A father like Gomez, who could blame her? Attila the Hun would be a better influence.

Beth said, "It only worked up to a point. Roberto thinks Adam's dead, and that I'm doomed as a heavy user, but he still wants to find me. He thinks I killed his son and he wants vengeance. In all the time I've known him, this is the one thing he hasn't been coldly businesslike about.

He won't stop till he's killed me, Carver, and now I don't wanna die. Whatever else you might think of me, I know I can be a good mother. Adam needs me. *We* need *you* if we're gonna make it through this. You might not like it, but that's the way it fell.''

Carver said, ''I'm no guarantee.''

''None of those in this life.''

''Who else knows the truth?''

''Only the doctor, who has every reason in the world not to talk. And my friend Melanie, who won't talk. A couple of people I was close to know I'm on the run and Roberto wants me dead. I talk to them now and then, and they tell me what they know about whatever he's doing. That's how I found out about you turning down Roberto's offer. Sometimes they don't know enough, though. I can't keep out of his path much longer.''

''Why don't you get far away from here? Out of the state?''

''Roberto has connections anywhere I'd go; drug trafficking is all about connections. And fear. And I don't have any family left. Melanie's closer to me than anyone; that's why she's hiding us at her place in Fort Lauderdale for a while.''

''If you're that close to Melanie, won't Gomez be watching her?''

''He doesn't know about her. Melanie used to be a coke addict. She went through rehabilitation and she's been clean for the past five years. Used to be a hooker, too, but now she's outa that game. That's where I knew her from. I cut her outa my life after Roberto because of the drugs. I knew she'd be back on coke and I'd be responsible. Then we met again at the university, when we were both taking a final. She's a secretary at a brokerage firm in Lauderdale. So I'd go see her every once in a while, but I kept her, and our friendship, a kinda secret. She understood. We'd talk about my life, but we'd skirt what it was my husband did to make money. I feel reasonably secure at her place, but I know I'm not completely safe, and I don't want anything to happen to Melanie because of this. But most of all, Carver, I want to save my baby. And I want you to help me.''

Carver said, "I don't know if I can.''

"I'm asking you to try. I'll pay you. Information and money, but you never can say where either came from.''

"What kind of information?''

"There's s'pose to be a big drug drop here in Del Moray soon.''

"How soon?''

"I don't know. Days, weeks. Not months.''

"Why don't you go to the law?'' he suggested. "Work a deal, Supply them with what they need to put Roberto away, and they'll set you up with a new identity, give you and Adam a chance.''

She shook her head violently, startling Adam, who squawked again. She fit the nipple back in his mouth and said, "You're speaking bullshit, Carver. I'll talk to you 'cause you're not the law and I'm desperate. That makes it personal. One thing you can't do with drug dealers at the top of the pyramid is go to the law and be an informer. The dealers got bought-and-paid-for government snitches— they got goddam *governments*—to help them track you down and make you pay. They consider it time and money well spent. It keeps others from informing. I'm gonna stay one of the others. The government witness protection program ain't for shit. If I talked to the cops or DEA, I'd be dead within a year or two years or five years, and so would Adam.''

"But Roberto figures you'll be dead within a few years anyway, as far gone as that doctor said you were on heroin.''

"So maybe he'll stop searching for me after a year or so. But if I talk, he and a lot of other people will *never* stop looking for me. They'll wanna be certain I'm dead. Not just so I can't talk anymore, but to discourage anyone else from playing close with the law.''

"You're between a rock and a rock,'' Carver admitted.

"And you're the only one I can trust. The only one I know who's refused to do something for Roberto, who's stood up to him.''

Carver said, "This isn't *Shane*."

"Damned right it's not. If it was, I'd just sit back and wait for the happy ending."

The tiny face among the blanket folds opened dark eyes and tried to focus them on Carver. Couldn't do it. Concentrated again on the bottle, which was now almost empty.

Carver said, "He's going through that milk in a hurry."

Beth was looking at him. Proud, unbroken, but desperate. Not just for herself. "You gonna help us, Carver?"

He said, "Give me a phone number where I can reach you and let you know. I've gotta think about this."

"But you *might* help?"

"Might, sure." He lent her his ballpoint pen and she printed her friend Melanie's phone number on the back of one of his business cards. He told her he'd call her sometime today or tonight. Tomorrow at the latest.

He leaned over his cane and stood up, then looked down again at Elizabeth and Adam Gomez, family unit. The smell of the sea was in the air, the primal stuff of life, of raw survival.

He started to limp away, then turned and said, "Cute kid."

She said, "I know."

15

CARVER HAD a connection at Florida State University, an entomologist named Fisk who'd helped him identify a certain type of beetle in a previous case. He phoned Fisk and had him check Student Records. Then he sat at his desk and sketched indecipherable shapes on his memo pad. Some of them looked like infants.

Within an hour the phone rang. Fisk. He told Carver there was indeed an Elizabeth Gomez of Fort Lauderdale registered at the university. She was in the correspondence program, six credit hours into her sophomore year, and carrying a 3.9 grade-point average.

Carver thanked Fisk and hung up. So far Beth Gomez had leveled with him. But so far wasn't very far.

He dragged his cross-directory from a bottom desk drawer and used it to match an address with the phone number Beth had given him in the park. The number was listed in the name of Melanie Beame of 242 Wayfare Lane, Fort Lauderdale. Beth's friend Melanie, just as she'd said.

Carver glanced at his watch. Past three o'clock, and Fort Lauderdale was over an hour's drive down the coast. Even if he left immediately, there wouldn't be much left of the day by the time he got there. On the other hand, what he had in mind might be better accomplished at night, so there was no rush.

He limped from the office, lowered himself into the sun-baked Olds, then drove to his cottage, where he stuffed a change of clothes and a shaving kit into his scuffed leather suitcase. Then he phoned Edwina, but she wasn't home. She wasn't in her office at Quill Realty either, and no one there knew how to reach her.

She seemed to be distancing herself from her employer as well as her lover, he thought, weakening her ties as she prepared to cut them. He tried to ignore the hollow sensation around his heart as he punched out her home number again and left a message on her machine, explaining he might have to be gone for a while on business and he'd call her soon as he returned. He said he's miss her, then added just before he hung up, "This is Fred, by the way." A joke. He wished he hadn't said it.

He locked the cottage behind him and tossed the suitcase in the back of the Olds. On the highway, he stopped at a Texaco station and bought gas, a quart of oil, and a pack of Swisher Sweet cigars.

The station's bell dinged twice as he ran over the signal hose on the way out. A guy in a greasy service uniform and holding a can of oil as if he were going to drink it glared at him, then poked his head back beneath the raised hood of a station wagon.

Carver turned left onto the highway to point the nose of the Olds south toward Lauderdale.

HE'D STOPPED for supper, and it was dusk when he checked into the Pelican Motel, off A1A. It was on a side road and not near the ocean, so it was inexpensive and saved him the time of trying to find a beachside motel with a vacancy.

The Pelican was a rehabbed old tourist court whose individual stucco cabins had been converted to duplexes. All except the first and largest cabin, which was office and living quarters. There was a fling stork painted on the sign by the road, and plastic pink flamingos perched on thin metal legs were stuck into the lawn in front of the office. On the wall behind the desk was a large oil painting of a heron standing on one spindly leg by the sea. Not a pelican in sight. The place probably wasn't owned or operated by ornithologists, but that was okay with Carver if the sheets were clean.

He registered and paid in advance, and the wry-faced old man behind the desk directed him to the end cabin, then handed him a key attached to a plastic tag in the shape of what looked like a seagull.

Carver drove the Olds to the far end of the gravel lot and parked it in front of the last in the line of small beige stucco cabins. There were only a few other cars parked at the motel, and he'd been told no one was staying in the other half of the cabin, so there'd be no loud TV or crying child to keep him awake. No late-night sounds of love-making to cause him to wonder what he was doing here instead of back in Del Moray with Edwina.

He lugged his suitcase to the cabin door, used the key, and pushed the door open with his cane. The air was hot and stale and smelled faintly as if someone had just stubbed out a cigarette. He flipped the light switch, then limped directly to the air conditioner jutting from one of the curtained windows and turned it on. It sounded as if it were trying to commit mechanical hari-kari, but it shoved out a steady current of cold air.

The cabin was even smaller than it appeared from the outside. There was room for only a double bed, a time-scarred oak dresser with a mirror, a rickety wooden chair, and a TV mounted on a metal bracket than angled from the wall. The tiny bathroom was incongruously modern: white fixtures, white tile, and a white fiberglass shower stall. Black cockroach scurrying out of sight behind the vanity. Carver shut the bathroom door and turned back to the main room. There was only one small closet, standing open, and a bolted connected door to the other half of the cottage.

He didn't bother unpacking, leaving his suitcase lying flat and unopened on the luggage stand at the foot of the bed. There was no way to know how long he'd be in Fort Lauderdale; might be a couple of hours, might be a couple of days. It depended on how things went at 242 Wayfare Lane.

He limped back down to the office and coaxed a Fort Lauderdale newspaper from a battered and stubborn vending machine, then asked the old guy behind the desk if he had a street map of Fort Lauderdale. He got no street map, but was told the drugstore a mile down the road sold that kind of thing and most any other item Carver might want. The old fella got so enthusiastic that Carver wondered if he owned part interest in the drugstore.

Carver returned to his cabin. It was too cool now; seemed the air conditioner's thermostat wasn't working. He turned the blower on low and stretched out on the creaking old bed, opened the newspaper, and read about the latest standoff between Congress and the White House, the Irish Republican Army killing a British trooper in Belfast, a man in Miami who'd set himself on fire to protest the rollback in civil-rights legislation. There sure were a lot of people out there with causes, but none with one so simple as that of Roberto Gomez, who had devoted himself to killing his wife. Carver turned to the comic strips and got a yuk out of "The Far Side," the only sane thing in the paper.

When it was completely dark outside, he left the cabin and drove to the drugstore the old man had told him about. It was a new brick building as spacious as an airplane hangar, with wide aisles and low counters stacked with merchandise. There were T-shirts, luggage, books and magazines, hardware, auto accessories, groceries, housewares, electronics. In one corner there were even drugs, some over-the-counter medicines and a prescription window. Carver bought a detailed Fort Lauderdale street map, then drove into town.

Even in the dark, it didn't take him long to find Wayfare Lane. It was in the west end of the city, a narrow street that wound beneath ragged palm trees and an occasional sprawling sugar oak.

Number 242 was a flat-roofed clapboard house set back on a small lot and surrounded by shrubbery. It was painted a pale color Carver couldn't identify by night, and had dark shutters and trim. Light edged out around closed drapes in a front window, where one of the shutters was twisted and dangled like a vestige of a prehistoric wing. The shrubs on the north side of the house were bathed in a faint yellow glow from a side window.

Carver eased his foot off the brake and let the Olds rumble slowly down the street until it had reached a point where he was half a block away but was able to see the lighted side window at an angle. He positioned the car just so, then killed the engine and got his 10 × 50 Nikon binoculars out of the glove compartment.

Slumped low in the seat so he'd be almost invisible in the dark, he focused the binoculars on the window.

There was a bookcase that contained a few books and a lot of stereo equipment and record albums. With the powerful binoculars, he could almost make out the names of some of the albums. A dial on the stereo system was glowing; there would be music in the house. The back of what looked like a brown chair was visible. Also a table with an orange lamp on it. Carver figured he was looking at about a third of the living room.

A shadow passed over the wall, and a slender, red-haired woman came into view. She stood before the stereo for a moment and adjusted something, maybe changed stations, then moved back out of sight. He got the eerie impression she existed only when he saw her in the window, like a character in a play.

With the infinite patience of his trade, Carver stayed where he was for over an hour. He caught a few more glimpses of the redhead. She was wearing a green robe with wide three-quarter-length sleeves, several gold bracelets on her left wrist. Her hair was pulled back and up and lay in a swirl on the crown of her head. She had a pale complexion that made her dark eyes and lipstick mouth vivid, and despite being too thin, she was attractive.

She didn't come into view very often, but her shadow was active on the wall. She seemed to sit down for short periods of time in the chair whose back was visible to Carver, then she'd rise and her shadow would flicker across the room.

He pressed the binoculars to his eyes and adjusted the focus as she came into sight again. She stood with her hands on her hips, then her body jerked and she looked toward the front of the house. Someone must be at the door. She moved off in that direction.

When he lowered the binoculars for a moment, he saw the man on the front porch. He drew the dark form into focus just as the door opened. The redhead—Melanie Beame, Carver assumed—stood framed in light that spilled outside to illuminate a short, stocky black man wearing a gray suit. Melanie moved back and he entered the house. The front door closed.

Carver aimed the binoculars again at the side window and saw nothing. Not even moving shadows.

Lowering the binoculars, he studied the layout of the neighboring houses and yards. There was a spot where he might conceal himself in some shrubbery in the yard next to Melanie's and have a more comprehensive view into the living room. It would be risky, but he didn't see that he had much choice.

He climbed out of the Olds. Had to stand for a minute and stretch his cramped back muscles before closing the car door quietly and limping away.

A few porch lights were glowing, but no one was on the dark street. He was sure he wasn't seen as he made his way over the neighbor's sparse lawn to the dense mass of shrubbery.

There were fragrant blossoms on the bushes, but no thorns. He settled down among the branches and brushed away an insect that skittered across his bare arm, almost dropping the binoculars, catching them by the strap. In the distance a dog was barking frantically, but Carver was sure it had nothing to do with him. The sweet scent of the blossoms tickled his nose, and for a moment he had to resist the urge to sneeze.

He glanced around at the darkness, then raised the binoculars to his eyes and focused on Melanie Beame's living room. He didn't like this kind of thing; it made him feel like a voyeur. He wouldn't want to try explaining his actions if someone saw him and called the police to report a peeping Tom.

Ah! He forgot his uneasiness as Melanie and the black

man came into clear view. There was a blanket-draped crib in the room, and Melanie leaned over it and lifted out a baby that looked like Adam Gomez, but Carver couldn't be sure. Infants tended to look alike to him, miniature old men with fat cheeks. This one had to be Adam, though. The black guy stood by Melanie and stared at the baby, then grinned and moved away.

Melanie put the baby back down. She fiddled around with it, then straightened up and stood for a moment staring down into the crib. The black guy came up behind her and gripped her waist with both hands, as if he might be trying to make his fingertips meet. She turned around, smiling, and he kissed her on the lips. It was a long kiss. Then Melanie and the black guy clung to each other for a while, until he pulled away, said something, and walked out of sight. She yanked the sash of her robe tight and went to the chair Carver could see of now, plopped down in it, and began reading a glossy magazine. Looked like a *Cosmopolitan*.

After about ten minutes her head jerked around and she laid the magazine, still open, on the table with the lamp. Carver knew what was going on; there was somebody else at the front door. He couldn't see the porch from here, so he stayed focused on the window.

This time it was Beth Gomez, wearing the same khaki pants and white blouse she'd had on when she'd talked to Carver. She said something to Melanie, then walked directly to the crib and gazed down at Adam. She bent low and looked as if she kissed him. Then she stood up straight and tucked in her blouse in back, causing her heavy breasts to strain against the material of the blouse. Carver could see now that Melanie was much shorter than Beth, probably no more than five feet tall, as the two women stood and talked.

They both turned around, away from him; the black guy must have come back into the living room, but Carver couldn't see him. Melanie walked out of sight. Beth sat down in the chair near the crib and crossed her legs. She picked up the magazine, then put it down almost immediately, as if it bored her. She sat there and stared at Adam.

Carver watched her until she got up and left the room. Lights winked on behind lowered shades in the rear of the house.

He let the binoculars dangle from their leather strap around his neck, grabbed his cane with both hands, and levered himself to a standing position. Listening to his own rapid breathing, he glanced around and then limped back to the Olds.

He sat for a while behind the steering wheel, listening to the screams of a thousand crickets and not moving, itching from the bushes and feeling a rivulet of perspiration trickle down the side of his neck.

So somebody else, the black guy, knew about Beth and Adam staying with Melanie. Beth hadn't told Carver everything. But she'd been truthful about the rest of it, he figured. She'd really taken courses at the university. And she'd taken a chance by giving him Melanie Beame's phone number.

He started the Olds, turned it around in a driveway, and returned to the Pelican Motel.

After draping a towel over the air conditioner's vents to stifle the flow of cold air into the chilled room, he slept nude beneath a single sheet.

Early the next morning, he lowered the Olds's canvas top and drove fast beneath a swollen gray sky to Orlando.

16

DESOTO WAS dressed in white today except for a pale blue tie: tropical white suit, white-on-white shirt. He sat relaxed behind his desk and smiled with very white teeth.

Carver limped over to the chair near the desk and sat down. Desoto swiveled in his chair and turned down the volume of his Sony; a forlorn Reuben Blades song continued its soft and syncopated Latin beat. The office was cool and smelled pungently like an office, as if somebody had just sharpened a dozen pencils and left the shavings lying about.

Carver crossed his good leg over his bad and said, "The Roberto Gomez thing's getting complicated."

Desoto arched his dark eyebrows, still smiling like a Hollywood Golden Era matinee idol. "How so, *amigo*?"

"The wife wants me to protect her from him."

"No complication there," Desoto said. "Don't do it."

"That's what I told her the first time she asked. Roberto thinks their baby died just after childbirth because the wife was carrying a secret heroin addiction. That's why he's got his troops our searching for her. Why one of them pumped a bullet into her sister, thinking she was Beth."

"Beth, huh?"

"Elizabeth Gomez."

"So what's the problem? She's hooked that hard on

horse, she'll be dead soon enough. Why doesn't he just forget her and let her waste away on her own?''

"He'd rather waste her himself. He's that type."

"Yeah, he would be. But I tell you, *amigo,* I don't feel sorry for her, only for the dead kid. Lie down with dogs, rise up with fleas. She got down with rats that carry death, but it was the kid that paid the price. Now let *her* pay. Sorta justice the police don't necessarily get involved in, but justice nonetheless.''

"The kid didn't die. I've seen him."

Desoto leaned forward and rested an elbow on his desk, cupping his chin in his hand. "What you trying to tell me, eh?''

"Beth Gomez lied to Roberto and used drug money to bribe her doctor to back her up."

"Why'd she do that?"

"She wants out of the drug life, for her baby and for herself. She thought Roberto'd think the baby was dead, and that she'd be dead soon enough, so he wouldn't look for either of them. She didn't realize how much he'd want revenge. Now she figures if she can manage to stay out of his way for a year or so, he'll cool off and stop searching. He'll think she's probably dead or worse off than dead.''

"Won't she be?"

"No. She's not on heroin; he only thinks she is. She's got no kinda drug habit."

Desoto sat back and considered. He took his chin out of his hand. "Hey, she's gotta be shitting you, *amigo.*"

"Why?"

"If she isn't hooked on drugs, she's addicted to the money that flows from them, and that's almost as powerful an addiction. It's in the blood just as surely. It's a lust that can't be denied. This woman was the whore of the scum of south Florida, my friend; do yourself a favor and see her as she is. Don't trust her."

Carver said, "She's not what you'd expect."

Desoto stared at him, as if comprehending something that was beyond Carver. "Christ!"

"I'm thinking mainly of the kid," Carver said.

"Gomez won't hurt the kid."

"Only raise him as a son."

"True, *amigo,* there is that."

"There's also McGregor. He read about my involvement with Gomez and he wants the lion's share of the action. He plans to run for mayor of Del Moray."

Desoto said, *"Sacro Dios!* He'll be the head of the rotting fish."

Carver said, "He told me to keep him tuned in, or he'll make life hard for me."

"He can do that," Desoto said.

"I know. Strait came to see me, too. He wants me to share all my secrets with the DEA."

"Strait might be a pain in the ass, but he's not like McGregor."

"Is anyone?"

"Maybe Roberto Gomez, only not so devious."

"McGregor wouldn't mind the comparison. He thinks being a cop's the flip side of being a crook."

"Sometimes that's the truth. He's proof of it." Desoto tilted back his head and seemed to be listening to the music. Voices were raised outside the office; a couple of detectives in an argument about a stakeout. "You came to me for advice," Desoto said. "I gave it to you. Let the drug woman and her child run the risks she's created."

"That what you'd do?"

"That's irrelevant."

"Why?"

"Because you'll do as you please, regardless of what I'd do."

Someone yelled for the arguing detectives to shut up, and they did. There was no noise from outside now except the relentless, ratchety whine of a dot-matrix printer. Song of the Orient.

Carver said, "I wanted you to know what's happening."

"So I might cover your ass if at all possible, eh?"

"Yes. And I'd like you not to mention the child's alive. Give him a chance."

"And the woman?"

"Give her a chance, too."

"I'll say nothing unless I have to. But the Belinda Jackson homicide investigation's still in progress, you know."

"You'll never be able to hang it on Gomez."

"Not yet, no," Desoto admitted. "But you're right, the child deserves a chance in the world."

"We all deserve that," Carver said. "Gives us the opportunity to fuck up on our own."

"Which is what you're doing if you cross people like Gomez and his friend Hirsh. They're the worst of the bad. A sadist, and one beyond sadism who'd cut on you as dispassionately as if you were filet mignon."

Carver uncrossed his legs and stood up with difficulty; his good leg had fallen asleep. He leaned propped on his cane. "I was sure you'd agree with me on the kid."

"I don't agree on the woman," Desoto said. "The high-rolling life she's led, the millions in drug money, it's like an unquenchable fire in the blood, even if she's not addicted to heroin. She'd have to be unusual indeed in order to change."

Carver said, "She's unusual."

Desoto half closed his eyes and said, "Are you really going to do this, *amigo*? Play the protector for a drug lord's wife and child?"

"I don't know."

Desoto shook his head sadly. He reached behind him and turned the Sony's volume back up. A mariachi band was strumming and shouting enthusiastically.

Carver left the office, limping with unmistakable Latin rhythm.

17

By the time Carver drove down the narrow road to his beach cottage, the Olds was running hot. He could smell the sweet scent given off by boiled coolant. The radiator was rusty and leaking, he was sure. He made a mental note to have it repaired before the old car left him stranded.

He parked alongside the cottage and switched off the engine. A few seconds passed, then steam billowed from beneath the hood, and the windshield fogged. Great. He hoped he hadn't pushed the car too hard and harmed the engine.

He climbed out and limped around to the front of the Olds. Worked the double latch and raised the long hood.

Heat rushed up and hit him in the face. He stepped back and watched more steam rise and dissipate in the already hot air. The motor was ticking loudly and something was hissing like an angry snake. Oh-oh!

He edged close and peered beneath the hood. A thread of water was angling from a break in the top radiator hose and spattering steamily on the inside of the fender well. Carver was relieved. He'd been lucky; replacing the faulty rubber hose was easier and cheaper than having the radiator repaired. It was a job he could handle himself in fifteen minutes.

He left the hood raised so the motor would cool faster,

then turned away from the mass of hot metal. He needed some air conditioning and a cold Budweiser, needed to sit down.

So preoccupied was he with the car that he didn't notice anything unusual as he clomped up the stairs onto the plank porch.

Until a voice said, "Nice to see you again, Mr. Carver."

Carver stopped, swiveled on his cane, and saw Hirsh standing on the end of the porch. He must have stepped around the corner of the cottage and scissored his long legs over the rail. He was wearing what looked like the same dark blue, vested suit. His hair was slightly mussed and he was sweating hard, but his sad blue eyes were calm, almost gentle. He was holding an Uzi submachine gun, not threateningly, but letting it dangle at his side casually, as if he'd been interrupted cleaning it.

Hirsh said, "Stay right there, please." He glanced to the side.

Gomez, wearing tight-fitting jeans, blue Avia jogging shoes, a blue T-shirt, and half a dozen gold neck chains, swaggered into view. He was smiling at Carver. He raised his right hand and waggled his fingers at someone out of sight around the side of the cottage, a combination wave and summons.

Carver heard an engine grind and kick to life, and a late-model black Ford pickup truck jounced into view over the rough ground. Gomez gave another hand signal, and the truck braked to a halt and sat with the motor idling. The driver was a Latino with a drooping dark mustache. He draped a wrist languidly over the steering wheel and sat staring straight ahead through the windshield. Might have been at an intersection, waiting for the light to change. There was a large metal barrel standing upright in the back of the truck.

Gomez made the same motion to Carver he'd first made to the driver of the pickup. "C'mon, Carver, you gotta fucking see this."

Hirsh didn't change expression, but he raised the compact and deadly Uzi a few inches. His sausagelike forefinger was crooked around the trigger.

Carver limped down off the porch and heard Hirsh follow. Gomez was already swaggering toward the back of the pickup, waving for them to come along.

The three of them stood near the back of the truck. Hirsh lowered the tailgate, all the while holding the Uzi steady and looking sadly at Carver with the resignation that grew with hard-earned wisdom.

The barrel in the truck was laced with holes. Hundreds of them. Carver recognized them as bullet holes, some of them entrance holes, some exit. The barrel had been riddled with large-caliber gunfire from a lot of directions.

Gomez said, "Can you get yourself up in the bed of the truck with that bum leg?" He sounded concerned.

Carver didn't answer. Using his great upper-body strength to raise himself onto the steel truck bed, he scampered noisily to his feet and planted the cane with care on the ridged metal. Hirsh held the Uzi off to the side and stepped up beside him, grunting softly with the effort.

"Open the barrel and look inside," Gomez said. "Go ahead." He spoke in an affable tone, but it was more than a suggestion.

Carver stared at the large, perforated barrel. It was black except where the bullets had separated paint from shiny silver steel. And clean. Maybe a hosed-out fifty-gallon oil drum. A fly crawled out of one of the round holes, buzzed in a circle, and entered another.

"Mr. Gomez gave you an instruction," Hirsh said in gentle reminder.

Carver held on to the side of the truck bed as he shuffled up to the barrel. Its metal lid was sitting on it loosely, a little off center. Gomez moved around to the side of the truck, as if he wanted to watch Carver's reaction to whatever was in the barrel.

"Got any guesses what's inside?" Gomez asked, obviously enjoying himself all to hell.

Carver's head was hammering. A stench rising from the barrel closed in around him. "I doubt those are air holes."

Gomez gave his *Huh! Huh!* laugh. "Get it over with, my man."

Carver lifted the lid and made himself peer inside.

Forced himself to look at the thing's dead face.

Not Beth Gomez. Not Edwina. Not anyone he knew.

A bald man with a beard. He'd been placed in the barrel
and then riddled with automatic-weapons fire. Some of the
bullets that had initially missed him, or hadn't penetrated
the other side of the barrel as they exited his body, had
ricocheted around inside and caused incredible damage.
His head and face were barely recognizable. So much bone
had been smashed that his body had a limp quality and
had settled toward the bottom of the barrel, like a human
pudding dotted with moving raisins that were actually
feasting flies. The dead, drained flesh was a ghastly gray.
Here and there, dried blood formed crazy patterns and set
off the whiteness of exposed bone.

Carver backed away, twisted his body violently, and
vomited over the side of the truck. Dust rose from the
impact of his recent lunch spattering on the hard ground.

He straightened up, feeling his trembling running
through the cane. Spat several times to try to get the bitter
taste from his mouth and wiped his lips with the back of
his hand. Gomez was grinning at him. Giggling softly.
Hirsh looked at Gomez, then at Carver. He smiled and
very faintly shrugged, as if sharing a joke: What ya gonna
do?—Roberto's such a character.

"Okay," Gomez said, "c'mon fucking down outa
there."

Carver gladly struggled down out of the sun-heated truck
bed. The steel seared his palms as he lowered himself to
the ground. It hadn't seemed that hot climbing up.

Gomez had moved closer. "We gonna have a fucking
talk, my man."

Carver didn't answer. He couldn't shake the vision of
the once-human thing in the barrel.

Gomez stared at him. *"Huh! Huh! Huh!* You want I
should explain about the guy in the barrel?"

When Carver still didn't answer, Hirsh said, "I betcha
he'd like an explanation."

Gomez said, "Well, what's in the barrel used to work
for me. I trusted the scumbag. Turns out he was more loyal
to Beth than to me. One of my people heard him talking

to her on the phone and told me about it. He fucking tried to dummy up when we questioned him as to where Beth was. So we put him in that barrel out in the sun, let him soak in his own juices for a while." Gomez grinned and shook his head. "But you know what? The son of a bitch fooled us. He died of a heart attack or something, so we never did get him to talk."

"Bad break for you," Carver said.

"Well, those things happen. What we did then," Gomez continued, "is we pumped him and the barrel fulla holes, hosed down the barrel and whatever leaked out, and loaded it onto the truck. Brought it here so you could see firsthand what happens to folks that try to fuck with me."

Carver said, "So some you feed to crocodiles, some you shoot in a barrel."

Hirsh said, "Alligators."

"Whatever," Gomez said. Without looking around, he motioned with his arm, and the driver put the pickup in Drive. Dust drifted as the truck pulled away. Carver listened to it shift gears as it made its way along the road to the highway. Gomez said, "My man's taking the barrel to a boat. It'll be loaded on board, and some heavy anchor chain'll be dropped inside on top of the dead scumbag. Then the lid'll be bolted on and the barrel will be dropped overboard out at sea. Nobody'll ever fucking find it."

"Efficient," Carver admitted.

"I'm that," Gomez said proudly. As if to illustrate the fact, the long black Lincoln limo with the tinted windows glided around the side of the cabin and parked where the truck had been. Heat waves danced from the exhaust of its idling motor.

"Why are you giving me this example of your business methods?" Carver asked.

Gomez said, "I wanted you to know—to fucking *feel*— the kinda thing's gonna happen to you if you don't play straight with me. You see, the guy in the barrel, he was heard mentioning your name on the phone. Shame is, he never lived long enough to tell us why. But if you got anything to do with Beth, or if I find out you know where she is and you ain't telling me . . . well, you'll wind up worse'n our friend that just left to go on his last ocean cruise.'' He put his hands on his hips, stuck out his chest as if he might actually emit a rooster crow. The gold neck chains caught the sun. "Now, Carver, this make a fucking impression on you?''

Carver said, "How couldn't it?''

Gomez cocked his head to the side. He elevated his wacky eyebrows as if he were puzzled. "You're a tough cocksucker, you know that? You puked when you looked in the barrel, but you didn't pass out. Lotta guys woulda fucking keeled over. And there you stand being sarcastic.''

Carver raised his shoulders slightly and let them fall. He wouldn't let this self-styled drug dictator know how shaken he was. He said, "It was his turn in the barrel.''

"Huh! Huh! Huh! That's good, Carver. This guy's a piece of work, ain't he, Hirsh?''

"Sure is, Mr. Gomez. But then so was the one in the barrel.''

Carver said, "He call you Mr. Gomez in private?''

"Not in private,'' Gomez said, "but this is business, so he's being a bit formal.'' He spread his hands palms out. "Just business, being done so you keep outa my personal life.''

Hirsh said, "I think you made your point, Mr. Gomez.''

Gomez said, "Sure hope so. Have I, Carver?''

"I feel we know each other better. But don't look for me to invite you over for barbecue.''

"Or me to ask you to go fishing,'' Gomez said. "We don't need to be friends, just fucking understand one another. That's so if you *are* in any kinda contact with my wife, you break it and stay away from her. She's got a fatal disease called Roberto Gomez, and if you get near her, you're sure to catch it.''

Carver said, "I understand you, Roberto.''

"Fine. Good. That means I accomplished the purpose of this visit. 'Cause *I* understand *you,* Carver. You're a hard-ass, but you ain't fool enough to dive into a blender for a no-good cunt like Beth. Mother Teresa maybe, but not Beth.''

Hirsh said, "Or maybe Madonna."

"Huh! Huh!" Gomez turned and swaggered toward the limo. He opened a rear door and climbed in as Hirsh moved to follow. Old pro Hirsh walked as easily backward as forward, still looking disinterested and keeping the Uzi aimed in the general direction of Carver.

He folded his tall body into the back of the limo after Gomez, making the same soft grunting sound he'd made when he'd climbed into the truck. He pulled the door shut after him. The long, gleaming car spun its rear tires and threw sand and rock as it drove away.

Carver looked over at the Olds. It had stopped steaming. He limped to it and slammed the hood shut. The hollow clash of steel reminded him of the barrel, causing his stomach to lurch and a rage that had been smoldering in him to flare into something white-hot and constant.

He hobbled around the mess he'd made on the ground when he'd vomited, then he clomped inside the cottage and rinsed out his mouth. He drank a cold Budweiser while he sat in his creaking director's chair and trembled. The barrel with the body in it might even now be sinking toward the ocean bottom, plunging faster and faster as sea water poured through the bullet holes.

Carver shook off the ghastly vision, but it wasn't easy. He drank another beer before he phoned Beth Gomez and told her he'd work for her.

| 18 |

CARVER HAD just hung up on Beth when McGregor called. His irritating voice oozed over the line and for some reason reminded Carver of the body rotting in the barrel. Corruption speaking:

"Seen Roberto Gomez lately, ass-face?"

"Not since we had our talk," Carver said. Lying to McGregor wasn't lying at all, more like tricking the devil out of possessing your soul.

"Well, some DEA agent name of Strait came by to talk to me about him."

Carver watched a large and wicked-looking wasp droning against the window that looked out on the sea, restrained by a barrier it would never understand. "Why would Strait wanna talk to you?"

" 'Cause of you, Carver. Your office is in Del Moray, and that means Gomez might turn up from time to time in my jurisdiction. The DEA keeps tabs on shitballs like Gomez, case they fuck up and leave themselves open for arrest. If that happens, Strait wanted to make sure he has the Del Moray department's full cooperation."

"And you assured him you were in his corner?"

"Why not? Lying to the DEA ain't a cardinal sin. Then we talked about you. He thinks you're an asshole just like I do."

"Well, that's the DEA for you."

"Oh, I dunno, in some ways they're pretty sharp."

Carver said, "They usually dress nice."

"I think they might be thinking straight here, Carver. There being an established connection between you and Gomez, he's almost certain to return, like flies to shit."

"Except I no longer work for him. We don't have anything to do with each other."

"You'll 'scuse me if I don't rule out the possibility you might fib, won't you?"

Carver said, "I don't excuse you for anything."

"How characteristically cruel. And I was gonna inform you Gomez talked to the Orlando police. He gave them his ironclad alibi. Played dumb behind his high-price attorney. Acted shocked about his murdered sister-in-law. And he was damned worried about his missing wife. He thinks whoever killed the sister wants to kill her. Not illogical, is it?"

Carver said, "Not at all. That's what I think, too. But I'm out of it, no longer even an interested party."

"Just make sure you *get* interested if you see Gomez again or learn anything about him or the missing wife. You ever see a picture of Mrs. Gomez?"

A test. "Sure. Gomez showed me a snapshot when he hired me."

"A nigger bitch. Makes you wonder, huh? I mean, a guy with all that money, he can have any woman he wants, and he mixes it up in the sack with a black cunt."

"My guess is he loves her."

"What makes you say that?" McGregor acted as if the possibility had never entered his mind. Probably it hadn't.

"He's searching for her, isn't he?"

"Like he'd search for a missing bag of coke. She's something belonged to him that disappeared, that's all."

Most likely McGregor was right about that, Carver thought, the supposed dead son aside. Men like Roberto Gomez didn't behave along the lines of Ward Cleaver.

McGregor said, "She probably knows lotsa tricks. Gives a great spit-shine, whatever her color. Anyway, it don't rub off, and she's a looker, nigger or not. Like that Vanessa Williams, used to be Miss America till she fucked up. Now, I'd go for some of that in a minute."

"The department's got you in the wrong job," Carver said. "You oughta be in race relations."

"Don't imply I'm a bigot, scuzzball. Maybe you don't like me just because I'm pale and blond. My only interest in Elizabeth Gomez's color is it should make her easier to find. This is a cunt used to the big money, and a black woman like that'll stand out like a raisin on white bread most places where big money congregates. She ain't gonna go to ground in no inner-city slum with the rest of her kind. Not for long, anyway."

Carver said, "Maybe she sings gospel."

"She don't. I checked. She's just another greedy ghetto black bitch, interested in getting rich and getting laid, in that order."

"You sure? She went out and got some education. She's an honor student."

"Probably fucked for her grades. They're all alike."

"Black women?"

"Women. Even Edwina Talbot, your real-estate lady friend. Someday you'll learn."

"Too bad you and Sigmund Freud never met."

"The sonuvabitch was alive, I'd run him in for writing pornography. I wasted enough time talking to you, fuckface. You remember what I said. And take care of yourself."

Carver was astounded. "You concerned about my welfare?"

"Fucking right. I want you to stay alive at least long enough to lead me to Roberto Gomez when he's got his pants down."

As soon as McGregor had hung up, Carver tapped the cradle button for a dial tone, then punched out Edwina's number with his forefinger.

She still wasn't home. He tried Quill Realty again, and the receptionist told him Edwina wasn't there, then interrupted herself to say she was at that moment walking into the office. She asked him to wait, Ms. Talbot would take the call at her desk.

Carver waited. The wasp had given up on the window and was circling in the middle of the room. Now and then it darted angrily almost straight up, then struck the ceiling and spiraled lower. Carver could hear it droning. He wished it would go back to the window.

A minute later there were a couple of clicks on the line and Edwina's voice said, "Fred?"

"How'd you know?"

"The receptionist recognized your voice." Edwina sounded harried, annoyed that she'd been interrupted on the job. "I can't make it tonight for dinner," she said.

"I wasn't going to ask you."

"Oh?"

"I called to tell you I have to leave town again for a while. I'm not sure for how long."

"Where you going?"

"It's better if you don't know. I don't want you connected with this in any way."

"More melodrama."

Carver thought about the corpse in the barrel and said, "Just like a movie." *Except with the smell and the horror and the forever sleep of real death.*

She paused, then said, "I'll have to give Jack Lester my answer on the Hawaii job."

"Yeah, I guess you will."

"Fred?"

He felt his throat constrict. He couldn't tell her he didn't want her to go. Not if *she* wanted to go. "I'll call you soon as I get back."

"I'll be waiting." She hung up hard enough to hurt his ear.

He unpacked the dirty clothes from his suitcase, from his short stay in Fort Lauderdale. After tossing them in a pile on the bed, he stuffed the suitcase with clean clothes.

He dug an old plastic milk bottle from the trash, rinsed out the sour-smelling white residue, then used the bottle to fill the Olds's radiator with water. The engine had cooled, but the split hose was still dribbling. He tied a rag around the split. Should do for a while.

After washing his hands, he put the suitcase in the trunk and drove to a service station on the highway, where he had the leaking radiator hose replaced. The mechanic was good; the job took even less than the fifteen minutes Carver figured he would have spent on it.

Carver drove to Edwina's house on the coast and let himself in the back door with his key. He made his way to the bedroom where they'd made love so many times. The window was raised a few inches and he could hear the ocean. He limped to Edwina's dresser and removed the top drawer.

A large, folded yellow envelope was fastened to the back of the drawer with masking tape. Inside the envelope was Carver's blue steel Colt .38 automatic.

He removed the gun and left the empty envelope taped to the drawer. Put the drawer back, then checked the Colt's clip and mechanism, smelling oil and metal as the gun snicked heavily in his hand. Making sure the chamber was empty and the safety on, he replaced the loaded clip and tucked the Colt in his waistband beneath his shirt. Death waiting to be used.

Before he left, he called Melanie Beame's house and talked briefly to Beth Gomez. Told her he was on his way.

19

CARVER DROVE into Fort Lauderdale and ran a few red lights. Cut suddenly up a one-way street, one eye on the road, the other on the rearview mirror. He spent fifteen minutes doing that kind of thing, being unpredictable as if he'd gone mad from the summer heat, until he was sure the Olds wasn't being followed.

Melanie Beame answered the door of the tiny frame house on Wayfare Lane. She glanced behind her as if waiting for some kind of signal before letting Carver limp inside.

Beth Gomez was standing in the middle of the living room. She was wearing Levi's and a yellow blouse, looking beautiful and fresh-scrubbed, her hair pulled back and tied with a yellow ribbon. If McGregor ever saw her in person, he'd know why Roberto Gomez had coveted her above other women.

She'd followed Carver's instructions and packed immediately and lightly. At her feet, as if worshipping her, lay a gray tweed Gucci suitcase.

She said, "This is Melanie, Carver."

Carver almost blurted out that they'd met, then he remembered the only time he'd seen Melanie Beame was through binoculars while spying on her in this very room. The bookcase cluttered with stereo equipment, the brown easy chair, the table and lamp, all looked familiar yet somehow different now that he was among them. As if objects in a painting had acquired dimension because he, Carver, had become a figure in the scene.

Melanie Beame looked the same, though. A too-thin redhead with a cadaverous yet undeniably pretty face. Carver couldn't help thinking she appeared as if she were still being ravaged by drugs. He told her he was pleased to meet her, then turned to Beth and asked if she was ready to leave.

"Not yet," she said. She walked to a fancy maple cradle in the corner and bent over it gracefully. The look on her face was something.

The son of Beth and Roberto Gomez must have been sleeping. She whispered to him softly, cooing mother-ese that Carver probably wouldn't have understood even if he'd been close enough to hear. He looked over at Melanie Beame, who was staring at Beth with red-rimmed blue eyes that glistened with tears. Carver hoped she wouldn't start crying. That might set Beth off. Not to mention young Adam.

Beth straightened up and turned to face Carver. Wiped her eyes daintily with a long and tapered forefinger. "You sure we can't take him?"

Carver said, "He'll be safer here. And you know how difficult it'd be to care for him and avoid Roberto at the same time."

"He's right, Beth," Melanie said, moving closer to Beth and speaking softly so as not to wake Adam.

She had on peculiarly scented perfume, Carver thought. Then he realized it was talcum powder he smelled. It had been years since he'd been around infants. His own. He didn't like to think of those years. His own son was dead; he hadn't seen his daughter since last fall.

Melanie said, "Don't worry, I'll take care of him as if he were my own."

Beth curled her fingers into fists, probably digging her long red nails into her palms. "Oh, I know that, Melanie. But, Christ, this is hard!"

"But it's the right thing to do, Beth. Adam'll be fine;

you just take care of yourself. Let Carver, here, take care of you. Know what I mean?''

Beth gnawed her lower lip. Nodded.

Carver limped over to the cradle and looked down at the dark, tiny infant huddled in a corner among scrunched-up blankets. Adam Gomez had a bald head except for a swatch of black hair over his left ear. He was curled on his side; Carver wondered if there was a similar patch of hair over the concealed right ear. He commented again that Adam was a good-looking kid, and meant it. The baby seemed to have all its parts and nothing jumped out as ugly, anyway.

Beth had moved over and was standing near Melanie, her hands still balled into tight brown fists. She took a few steps toward the cradle, then stopped as if she'd come to the edge of a drop. Her shoulders lifted and expanded as she drew in breath.

After a few seconds she exhaled in a low sigh, spun around, and with an obvious effort of will snatched up her suitcase and walked to the door without looking back at her child.

Melanie caught her at the door and the two women embraced. Melanie was crying now, but Beth seemed to have control of herself. She knew better than anyone that this was life or death for her, and one world or another for Adam.

Melanie said, ''Goddammit, Carver, you better take good care of this lady.''

Carver said, ''Things'll work out.'' Though he wasn't so sure.

''You have my phone number,'' Melanie reminded Beth. ''You need to put your mind at ease about Adam, call me anytime.''

Beth swallowed hard, tried to speak but merely croaked. She bowed her head and moved out onto the porch.

She walked slowly across the street so that Carver could keep up. He took her suitcase from her, unlocked the Olds's cavernous trunk, and hoisted it inside. Got his own travel-scarred leather suitcase from the backseat and laid it next to the tweed Gucci. It looked like a worn-out bum who'd sneaked into bed with a countess. There was an airline luggage tag attached to the handle of Beth's suitcase, with her name and address scrawled on it.

Carver tugged at the tag until the elastic loop attaching it to the suitcase handle snapped. The damn thing whipped around and stung the back of his hand. He crumpled the stiff paper tag and tossed it out of sight in the shadows of the trunk, then slammed the trunk closed.

He opened the passenger-side door for Beth. She seemed to expect it. Sliding her shapely rear backward into the Olds, she pressed her knees tightly together and swung her long legs up and sideways.

Wondering if women practiced getting into cars that way, Carver closed the door. He limped around the Olds and lowered himself in behind the steering wheel, then bent forward and twisted the key in the ignition. The powerful engine ground, caught, and roared. It had barely caught its mechanical breath when he shoved the transmission lever into Drive. The tires *eeeped!* on hot pavement. He figured the sooner they got away from Wayfare Lane, the better jump they'd have on the future.

Beth couldn't help it; she glanced back at the house as the car pulled away.

Carver peeked, too, in the mirror.

Melanie was standing on the porch and waving as if she'd never see her friend again.

And maybe she wouldn't.

20

HE TOOK Interstate 95 north, then cut west. The top was up on the Olds, but the air conditioner wasn't working, so all the windows were cranked down. Air crashed and swirled through the car and ballooned out the canvas top as if it were inflatable. Carver drove fast, eyes fixed on the highway that narrowed in perspective to a thin, pinched break in the flat landscape wavering in the heat.

Almost shouting to be heard over the boom of the wind, Beth said, "Where we going on this date?"

She'd taken a shot at humor even in her predicament; Carver liked that. He continued staring straight ahead, both hands on the steering wheel. "Place called Dark Glades."

She digested the information. "That a town?"

"It thinks so." While on a case a few years ago, Carver had stayed in the swamp town of Solarville and thought it was backward and isolated. But on the drive back to civilization he'd passed through Dark Glades, and all of a sudden Solarville seemed progressive.

Beth knew they were driving toward the Everglades. "This Dark Glades one of those backwater swamp places?"

Carver said, "It won't remind you of Miami."

"Not the kinda surroundings I been used to, Carver."

"That's the idea."

''You think Roberto's not smart enough to figure I'd try
to fool him by running someplace I wouldn't ordinarily
go?''

''Got nothing to do with smart,'' Carver told her.
''Roberto will assume you think like he does, with the gut
instead of the brain. *He* wouldn't stay in a dump and eat
fish heads to stay outa harm's way, because he's too arrogant. He's got no idea you wouldn't react the same way.''

''You say fish heads?''

''Figure of speech. Anyway, this makes sense. Does
Roberto underestimate you because you're a woman?''

''Sure. It's built into a guy like that.''

''Uh-huh. That what made you think you could get by
with this in the first place?''

''That's part of it,'' she answered immediately, as if
she'd given the matter a lot of thought. ''The other part
was pure desperation.'' She flexed her long, dark fingers,
as if they'd become stiff and needed the knuckles loosened. Out of the corner of his eye, he saw her glance over
at him. ''You underestimate me because I'm a woman,
Carver?''

''Probably.''

Beth was silent for a long time. Then she said, ''You're
most likely right with this choice of hideaways, Carver,
but I'm not gonna like this.''

''You might change your mind. It's rustic.''

''Back in Chicago, rustic means old.''

He said, ''Old's what I want us to live to be.''

THEY REACHED Dark Glades just before nightfall. Even in
the soft dusk, the flat-roofed wooden buildings lining Cypress Avenue, the main street, didn't seem rustic. They
looked ancient and ready to collapse beneath the weight
of their years. The swamp humidity had turned whatever
colors the wooden buildings had been painted to a dreary,
mottled gray. The only brick buildings Carver saw were
the combination fire department and police headquarters,
a small restaurant, and the office of an auto-repair shop
with a couple of gas pumps standing outside it like bored
sentries. The Olds was the only vehicle moving on the

roughly paved street. Several old cars and pickup trucks were parked on the gravel shoulder or angled in front of some of the small shops. Half a dozen pedestrians, the men rough-looking in cut-off shirts with jeans or denim overalls, stood slouched on the edge of the road and stared at the Olds. A strange car usually meant fishermen from outside town, or maybe some lost motorist. Or trouble.

Beth said, "Pissant place don't even have a Mc-Donald's." Though she spoke better English than Carver did, she'd let herself ease into occasional echoes of street dialect on the hot and exhausting drive. She was more comfortable with him now. Less guarded. Maybe she liked him. He wondered why he thought that. What difference did it make?

"There's where we can dine out," he said, motioning with his head toward the restaurant.

"I dunno if I wanna eat at a place called Wiff's," Beth said dubiously.

"It's 'Whiffy's,' " Carver corrected her. "See, part of the neon sign's burned out, but it's lettered there on the window."

"Yeah, right near the dusty fern." She pointed at a leaning clapboard building with a sign over its door. "Looka that, there's moss on City Hall."

Carver looked. Sure enough, the flimsy structure was the city hall, and sure enough there was a greenish film of moss near the roof on the north side. There was also moss on a statue of what looked like a World War I dough-boy standing erect and aiming a rifle. Might even have been moss on the old man slumped on the bench near the statue.

As they neared the edge of town, the buildings became even more rundown, and many of them were up on stilts and in the shade of towering cypress trees.

Beth said, "Must flood a lot around here, people gotta live up in the air."

"Keeps the alligators out," Carver told her.

The road outside town became narrower and paved with gravel. It was raised a few feet above the level of the swamp water, flanked by tall saw grass and trees with exposed, gnarled roots that resembled massive, bare vines. Insects droned almost deafeningly and the air was suddenly cooler.

Carver saw a wooden sign up ahead; the Casa Grande Motel was where he'd remembered it. Soon another sign came into view, shaped like a Spanish castle and outlined in neon.

As he made a sharp right turn and parked near the office, Beth said, "I can't like alligators."

"Takes another alligator," Carver said.

When he switched off the engine, she seemed surprised. She must have thought he'd driven into the lot to turn around. She studied the motel through the windshield, then said, "Oh-oh. This it?"

"It," he confirmed. He knew how she must feel. The Casa Grande was a U-shaped stucco building with mock-Spanish decor. Ornate wrought-iron window grilles, a sun-faded red tile roof, heavy wooden doors. It had been white but was now a grayish color splotched with yellow where the stucco had been patched; webbed with cracks and exposed lathing where broken stucco had been ignored. Now that the car's motor wasn't running, the screaming and grinding of insects was even louder. The swamp grew close to the back and sides of Casa Grande, seeming to loom over it as if waiting for it to surrender to time and vine so the ground on which the motel sat could be reclaimed. There was a battered green Chevy pickup parked near the farthest end unit, a big, dark Harley-Davidson motorcycle parked close to it. Near the center of the low stucco building, a rapacious vine laden with dark red blossoms seemed to be gradually but surely devouring the building. It had once been confined to a trellis, but now only rotting, splintered remnants of fragile wood spindles remained visible, here and there protruding like bleached bones from the mass of waxy-looking leaves.

Carver sensed Beth's apprehension. He said, "It's nicer inside."

"Ever stay here?"

"No," he admitted.

"Then how do you know it's nicer inside?"

"Must be."

He opened the car door and set the tip of his cane in the gravel. Levered himself up and out from behind the steering wheel so he was standing beside the car. The warm air was humid enough to grab by the handful. It carried the fetid, sulfurous smell of the swamp. Carver glanced around at the green isolation. He bent down over the cane slightly so he could see Beth, still inside the car, and said, "I'll go make sure they have a vacancy."

"You taking any bets?"

He ignored her and limped toward the office. He was perspiring heavily and his clothes were stuck to him. A film of sweat clung to his face like a mask. A cloud of gnats followed him; he had to wave them away from his eyes and nose.

A large black-and-yellow butterfly of a type he'd never seen lay fluttering feebly on the wooden steps to the office door, being devoured by huge red ants. Carver stepped on the unfortunate insect to end its misery, then kicked the mess, including some of the ants, aside. A weathered sign on the office door said FREE COFFEE AND DONUTS EVERY MORNING. He pushed the door open with his cane, gripped the wooden doorjamb, and moved inside.

The office was small, painted dead white, probably to make it appear larger. There was a single, blue vinyl-covered chair, a table with a Mr. Coffee on it, and a wooden wall rack of the sort usually stuffed with tourist brochures. This rack was empty.

The registration desk looked homemade out of cheap lumber. It was painted white, like the walls, over a rough sandpaper job, and had a top covered with speckled linoleum. An old GE air conditioner mounted high on the back wall had the office cold enough to chill beer, and the bearded little man behind the desk sat as perfectly still as if he'd been frozen. But his eyes moved, watching Carver.

Carver said, "Got a vacancy?"

The bearded guy smiled and stood up. Or down. When he slid off his stool, his chin was barely higher than the desk. He said, "A single?"

"No, my friend's in the car. Two rooms next to each other, with a connecting door."

The man gave Carver a neutral look. "No hitch, I can do that. Thirty a night each."

"Good enough."

"Got a credit card?"

"I'll pay cash in advance. We'll be here about a week. Maybe longer." Carver reached in his pocket and dragged out his wallet. He peeled off three hundred-dollar bills and laid them on the desk. An offering to no-questions-asked commerce.

The bearded man said, "Well, glad to have a guest like you. Whatever your reason for being in Dark Glades." He waited for Carver to toss back the conversational ball. When there was no response, he picked up the bills and laid a registration card on the desk. He said, "My name's Eddie Watts. Just Watts is what I'm called, though. I be of any help, you lemme know."

Carver finished signing the card, using his real name. Why not? If Roberto Gomez traced them this far, he wouldn't be thrown by a Smith or a Jones on a motel register. But Carver signed Beth in simply as "and friend." Some sort of subconscious sense of chivalry? Protecting her reputation, for God's sake? *Do you underestimate me because I'm a woman?*

Watts rotated the card so he could read it. He had scraggly blond hair, though his beard was black. A wide, amiable face. Blue eyes whose pupils somehow seemed dusty and dulled. He squinted out the dirty office window at the car and said, "Your friend's black." As if Carver might not have noticed.

"That a problem?" Carver asked.

Watts shook his head. "Not with me. Got some real rednecks in Dark Glades, though. Not to mention stiff-necked religious folks that ain't all that tolerant."

"We'll spend most of our time in our rooms," Carver said.

Watts tried hard not to give him the wrong kind of smile, and couldn't help shooting another glance out the window. He said, "Sure. Like I said, lemme know if you need anything.'' He handed Carver two keys attached to green plastic tags. A third key with a red tag. "The red one fits the connecting door. Other two are to rooms six and seven, right near the center of the building. Best I got. Icemaker and soda machine right nearby.''

Carver decided to let Watts assume a romantic motive for the stay at Casa Grande. It would be more believable and less disturbing than the truth. He laid a fifty-dollar bill on the desk and said, "My friend and I wanted to get away and enjoy being by ourselves for a while. You understand. If anybody comes around asking about either of us, will you let me know?''

Watts laid his palm over the fifty and made it disappear as if he were demonstrating sleight of hand. "Glad to extend the courtesy, Mr. Carver.''

Carver gripped the keys in his free hand and limped toward the door. Behind him Watts said, "I myself don't care a whit about color. Think black's rough, try being five feet tall.''

Carver knew Watts would have to stretch high on elevator shoes to top five feet, but he said nothing. It was self-deception that made life tolerable, so why fuck with it when it was harmless?

As he stepped outside, the sauna-like heat folded itself around him. He got in the car, drove down to cabin 6, and backed into a parking slot. "The guy at the desk has the impression we're lovers,'' he said.

Beth was sweating. Her hair had come partly down to curl darkly in front of her ears. Even her gold loop earrings seemed to be drooping. When he turned off the engine, she said, "Carver, it's not like I don't appreciate—''

He cut her off by handing her the key to 6. "There's a connecting door we keep unlocked. We can also keep it closed.''

She nodded. "I'm sorry I assumed, but you know how it is.''

"Yeah.'' He climbed out of the car and opened the trunk. She reached in quickly and pulled out her Gucci suitcase. He looked around at the looming green swamp and the narrow gravel road. Some sort of brown-and-gray bird with long, spindly legs was standing near the road, studying him with cocked head. It made a throaty clucking noise he'd never heard a bird make before. Carver got out his own suitcase and slammed the trunk lid. "Let's settle in, then get some supper."

"Sounds right. Just give me time to take a shower."

He waited until she was inside, then unlocked the door to 7 and limped in. Warm, stale air gave way for the fetidness of the swamp pushing in around him.

Actually, the room *was* better than the outside of the motel suggested. It was small and clean, with a double bed, an old walnut chifforobe instead of a closet, and a new-looking K-mart-brand color TV; an oak nightstand and an orange ceramic reading lamp were on each side of the bed. There was a dimestore print of a desert landscape on the wall over the brass headboard. The bathroom had black and white hexagonal tile on the floor, a tub with an added-on shower attachment and plastic curtain, a toilet bowl that was cracked but apparently didn't leak, plenty of towels and soap. There was a full roll of toilet paper, and a spare tucked in the plumbing beneath the washbasin. Sun poured through the single small window in the bathroom, and everything smelled like pine-scented disinfectant.

Near the bed was an air conditioner like the one in the office, protruding from the wall. Carver hobbled across the worn but clean gray carpet, switched the unit on, and slid the thermostat over to High. It was noisy but seemed to work okay.

He went to the connecting door and unlocked it, leaving the key in it. There was a sliding-bolt lock as well as the lock in the doorknob. It had been painted over years ago, when the door had been enameled white, and was stuck; it took him a while to force the bolt free and unlock it. Probably there was another one just like it on the other side. Carver didn't try to open the door.

Plumbing rattled in the walls and water hissed. Beth running her shower.

Carver lugged his suitcase over to the bed, opened it,

and got out some fresh underwear and socks. He placed the Colt in one of the chifforobe drawers.

He got undressed, then went into the bathroom to take his own shower.

Beth yelped on the other side of the wall as he twisted the faucet handle and water spewed over him. There was a frantic banging on the wall. A faint voice. "Carver, you turned your shower on and my water stopped!"

He picked up the tiny, lilac-scented bar of motel soap and lathered his arms and chest, pretending not to hear.

| 21 |

Beth's shower was still running as Carver toweled dry and limped from the bathroom. The short-napped gray carpet was rough under his bare soles. It was cool in the room and felt good. He sat on the edge of the bed and dressed himself, then scooted around until he could reach the old-fashioned black phone on one of the nightstands. Dialed 9 for an outside line.

McGregor wasn't on duty at Del Moray police headquarters. Carver hung up. Dialed 9 again, then McGregor's home number. Got an answering machine.

When the high-pitched tone sounded to signal him to begin his message, he said simply, "This is Carver."

Click. McGregor was home and had been screening his calls. "Got something for me?" his voice said.

"It's possible."

"This line sounds funny. Where you calling from?"

"Doesn't matter."

"If it didn't matter I wouldn't have asked, fuckface. You better not cut up cute with me or—"

"Did I hear you say *you* had something for *me*?" Carver interrupted. He was tired of McGregor's threats; he already knew he was dealing with something sick and vicious with a badge.

McGregor sighed loudly; it was a lonesome sound on

the already hissing connection. "All right, I'll play your game. You want me to say please with sugar on it? Grow the fuck up, Carver!"

A series of sharp raps sounded from the closed connecting door. Beth was working on the painted-over sliding bolt lock on her side, maybe using a shoe for a hammer.

McGregor said, "You at a carpenters' convention?"

"Just a minute."

McGregor objected to Carver leaving the phone, but Carver didn't listen to what he said. A barrage of tinny obscenity trailed faintly from the receiver as he laid it on the nightstand.

Carver got up with the help of his cane. Limped over and pounded on the door a few times with the heel of his hand. Kind of hurt, but he loosened the door where it had been painted to the frame. He heard Beth curse, more sharp rapping coming from near the bolt lock, then a metallic scraping sound. Carver twisted the doorknob. Felt it come alive in his hand as it rotated from the other side. He yanked backward and the door made an odd popping sound and swung open.

Beth was standing with a high-heeled shoe in her right hand. He'd identified the rapping sound correctly; she'd been using the shoe as a hammer on the bolt lock. She looked as if she wanted to use it the same way on Carver. She was wearing faded designer jeans and a blue short-sleeved blouse. White Reeboks. Still had on her gold loop earrings. She said, "This sure as hell isn't the Dark Glades Hilton, Carver."

He said, "Yes it is."

She strode into his room like a queen claiming property rights, immediately noticing the phone off the hook. "I interrupting?"

"No, better if you hear."

Beth stood with her long arms folded as Carver returned to the phone and lifted the receiver; he wondered if she realized how it emphasized her breasts. "Still there?"

"I'm still here," McGregor said. "Your main squeeze got a problem?"

"Not anymore." If McGregor thought Beth's voice belonged to Edwina, fine.

"So what's this conversation about, asshole?"

Carver glanced at Beth. "Roberto Gomez. I know for sure he tried to kill his wife and killed her sister instead."

"He pull the trigger?"

"No, but it was his man on the roof, acting under Roberto's orders."

"Why would he want to kill his wife? Even guys like Gomez don't often do that when they been jilted. They stop to think about it, realize cunt's replaceable."

"Doesn't matter why. I'm telling you he can be nailed for it."

McGregor was quiet for a while. Then he said, "Who was the shooter, that guy Hirsh?"

"Not Hirsh. It was one of a number of soldiers Gomez has out looking for his wife."

"Gomez has killed before, Carver. He's smart enough to arrange for cover. Has an alibi in this case, in fact. He told it to the Orlando police."

"It's a phony."

"Hell, yes, it is. But that don't matter if it can't be disproved."

"Point is," Carver said, "he's gonna keep looking for her. He's getting desperate, and desperate means careless. You stay on his ass, you'll be able to nail him for murder or something else. He's not himself these days. His judgment's clouded."

"Yeah, he hired you."

Carver looked at Beth. He was going to give McGregor the plum now. "There's also rumor of a drug shipment supposed to be smuggled into the country via Del Moray."

"Really now?" McGregor's voice took on a different frequency. "When?"

"I'm not sure. Soon, though." Carver glanced at Beth. She rolled her eyes as if she was scared. He realized she wasn't kidding.

"That it?" McGregor asked.

"All I've got for now."

"What do you expect in return for this, Carver?"

Carver said, "Nail the son of a bitch." Hung up.

Beth stared at him for a while, then said, "Well." Not a question.

Carver said, "The man I talked to is named McGregor. He won't say where he got the information on the drug drop. He can't."

"He a cop?"

"Yeah, but not in the way most people think of cops. He's the one you saw leave my office the day we met at the marina."

"Nobody's gonna arrest Roberto and make it stick, Carver. You're only jerking yourself off if you think so."

"McGregor might. He doesn't use orthodox methods. He'll plant evidence on him if he has to."

"That's been tried. The crooked cop's youngest child was murdered and the evidence disappeared. Cop wouldn't testify against Roberto and the charge was dropped. Roberto'll get down lower than anybody you put on his trail."

"Nobody can get lower than McGregor. He's at the bottom of the ocean, feeding on what sinks."

"He'll be there with weights on as part of the food chain unless he's careful." She sat down on the bed. Her denim jeans made a swishing sound as she crossed her legs. She smelled fresh, like the lilac-scented soap in the Casa Grande showers. "That our plan, to hide out here until your friend McGregor puts a collar on Roberto?"

"More or less."

"Piss-poor one."

"We can improvise as we go."

Beth made herself smile. "Better'n where we were yesterday," she said.

"That's the idea," Carver told her, "a day at a time, until the situation changes." He leaned on his cane and looked down at her, into her dark eyes. "How do you feel about Roberto going up for life? Maybe being executed?"

Her face was a mask, but her eyes seemed to absorb all the light in the room. "The longer I lived with Roberto, the harder it got for me to deny what he was. Or what I was. I knew what was buying the kind of life I was leading. But I didn't know how to escape; you don't walk out and send around your divorce lawyer with a man like Roberto. He regarded me as *his*. Still does. Then I got pregnant and I knew I had to at least *try* to get out. Not just for me, but for my child's future.''

''Roberto's child, too.''

''That's what scares the shit outa me, Carver.''

He poked at the carpet with his cane. It was almost thread-bare, and the cane's tip didn't leave an indentation. ''Nothing left between you and Roberto?''

''Nothing good. Hasn't been for months. Christ, Carver, he just killed my sister and it was supposed to be me!'' She swallowed so hard he could hear saliva crack in her long throat. She looked the way she had as they were leaving Melanie Beame's house, as if any second she might break and begin sobbing.

But she knew she didn't have the luxury of tears; all her energy was needed for survival, and not just her own.

She exhaled heavily, puffing out her cheeks, and stood up from the bed. He envied the ease with which she gained her feet, the liquid way she moved. ''I wanna call Melanie. Check up on Adam.''

Carver said, ''Fine.''

She went back into her room, hips swaying, and left the connecting door standing open. After a moment he heard her talking on the phone. He didn't know what she was saying and didn't want to eavesdrop.

When she came back her eyes were moist, but that was the only hint of emotional storm. She had hold of herself, this one. She'd reached down and found what she needed, what she hadn't known for sure was there. Not having a choice did that to people. Carver knew.

She said, ''Let's go revel in the local cuisine.''

He thought that was a good idea. And he hoped wherever they ate served liquor. He'd set a beast to catch a beast, and he needed a drink.

22

WHEN THEY went outside to get in the Olds, Carver noticed the big Harley-Davidson cycle was gone. The rusty old pickup truck had been joined by a late-model Chevy with a scrape along the left side from headlight to taillight. Not many Cadillacs or BMWs in Dark Glades; mostly ancient or battered domestic iron. The economic expansion touted by politicians hadn't reached into the swamp.

Carver saw the big Harley outside Wiffy's Restaurant and parked next to it. In the lowering dusk, heat was radiating in waves from the motorcycle's recently raced engine. The restaurant's broken neon sign was on and buzzing now, though it wasn't yet dark. A couple of moths were fluttering around it as if fooled by the noise and feeble light.

Whiffy's was surprisingly large inside. Up front was a wide area of square gray Formica tables and the kind of molded plastic chairs—some red, some blue—found in waiting rooms. To the left, beyond the chairs, was a long serving counter with high stools. Opposite the counter were wooden booths with straight, high backs. On the back wall was a mounted blue marlin above a lineup of video machines that were zinging and boinging in soft electronic cacophony.

Two men sat on stools near the front of the counter,

eating cornbread and beans and drinking beer. Another, older man was slumped at the far end, hunched over a cup of coffee. A tall, skinny man in Levi's and a sleeveless red T-shirt was coiled in front of one of the video games, scrawny arms tensed and hands darting to punch the buttons that would bring the desired results on a screen where something resembling a hockey game was portrayed in dots and flashes.

Carver and Beth sat down at a table near the front. There were a few crumbs on the gray Formica. A few flies. A black-and-chrome napkin holder, glass salt and pepper shakers, a half-full Heinz Ketchup bottle. Four large paddle fans with clusters of light fixtures slung beneath them were slowly rotating near the ceiling. Carver could feel the faint breeze. An air conditioner was humming somewhere, keeping the place fairly cool but not doing so much to keep the humidity out; that was probably impossible, so close to the swamp.

The rubber tip of Carver's cane didn't grip the slick linoleum, so he hooked its crook over the back of the chair next to him. The linoleum was gray with a kind of lighter gray cloud pattern on it, buckled in places. It creaked and made a sticky suction sound beneath the shoes of the short, dumpy young blond girl who'd been standing behind the counter and was now waddling toward them carrying two glasses of water. A couple of menus were tucked between her fleshy right arm and her ample chest. She was wearing cut-off jeans, and a white T-shirt that was lettered WHIF-FY's in black across the chest, above what looked like an ironed-on bat and baseball half hidden by the sag of her breasts.

She had a round, kind face, a nice smile except for bad teeth. She placed the glasses and menus on the table. "Hi, I'm Marlene. Getcha somethin' to drink?" *Bwip-bwip-zoing!* went the video game, much louder.

Carver said, "Budweiser if you got it."

"We got it. This ain't *that* far off the beaten path."

"Just water for me," Beth said.

Marlene went back behind the counter to get the beer while Carver and Beth studied the handwritten menus. One of the men at the near end of the counter turned and stared openly at Carver, then at Beth. He was fat and wore bib overalls and no shirt. Thick-soled brown leather boots. His sandy-colored hair was chopped so short he looked almost bald. There was a roll of flesh at the back of his sunburned neck. His eyes were sunk deep in pads of flesh and glared out at the world like the tiny, primitive eyes of pigs irritated on a hot day.

The man on the stool next to him was wearing jeans and a sleeveless T-shirt, like the guy at the video machine, only his shirt was white. He was tall, lean, and long-muscled. Tendons in his forearms rippled as he forked in a mouthful of beans. He didn't look in Carver's direction, just kept eating, chewing with his mouth open.

Marlene returned and Carver ordered the chicken-fried steak special. Beth asked for a hamburger and home fries.

When Marlene had gone, Beth said, "That fat creep at the counter keeps staring at me."

Carver poured beer in his glass, watched it foam, then looked to the side. "Not now, he's not. He's concentrating on his cornbread."

"Well, he doesn't look like he could concentrate on more'n one thing at a time. Wait'll he swallows, he'll look back over here."

"Probably'd like to ask you for a date."

"Fuck you, Carver."

"Such spirit."

She sipped her ice water daintily, little finger extended. Mouth didn't match manners. "Listen, Carver, what do you think this McGregor character can really do to catch Roberto?"

"Whatever needs doing. He'll see that the Del Moray marina and any likely landing sites along the coast'll be watched like a clock at quitting time. He'll take part in it himself, sleep in his car if he has to. The man's fucked up. Wants to be mayor."

Beth smiled. "You notice everybody wants to be what they're not?"

Carver sampled his beer. Good and cold. "You're no exception."

"Yeah, I know. What about you?"

He set the glass down in its puddle of condensation on the smooth table. The video game *bwipped* and *zoinged* some more. "During the last couple of years, I got divorced, got shot, lost a son, and got involved with a woman too much like me. What with my leg, the way my life took a turn, I approach things a day at a time."

"Like a recovering addict."

"Something like."

"What woman you involved with, Carver?" She was tactful enough not to ask about his son.

"Private matter," he said. "Anyway, it's not going good for us right now." *Bwip! Zoing!*

"I figured."

He didn't ask her how. It was better to leave Edwina out of anything that went on between them. He didn't like the way Edwina was changing in his mind, leaving him helpless and lonely, with terrifying moments when he could feel time flowing around him and carrying him like the current of a great river.

Beth said, "You got a lotta faith in your friend Mc-Gregor."

"He's not my friend. Not anybody's. That's the way he likes it, so he can sacrifice anyone he wants in whatever game he's playing."

"Sounds like a total jerk."

"He is. But he's good at what he does. He'll haunt the Del Moray coast like the Ancient Mariner."

"Well, he better stoppeth more'n one in three if he's gonna get the goods on Roberto."

The fat man at the counter said, "Marlene, put on some music, why doncha, so we don't have to listen to that goddam video machine fartin' at us."

" 'Kay, Junior." Marlene pushed through some swinging doors. Speakers mounted up near the ceiling crackled to life. Dolly Parton started singing about a party right next door. The man at the video machine hadn't turned around. He was still trying to influence microchips with body English.

A red light flashed on the video screen and an electronic

voice yelled "Score!" above the sound of Dolly's. Fat
Junior said, "Jesus H. Christ, I hate them 'puters!"

Marlene was back behind the counter, carrying plates
on a tray out in front of her with both hands. She said.
"That ain't no computer."

"Same fuckin' difference, ain't it?"

Marlene ignored his question and moved out from behind the counter. Squish-squished across the buckled linoleum and placed the plates of steaming food in front of
Carver and Beth. Carver was surprised; everything looked
delicious.

"Getcha anything else, jus' lemme know," Marlene
said, and turned and walked away. Her legs were thick
and brown beneath her cut-off jeans. Muscular rather than
fat. A tightness moved in Carver's groin and he averted
his eyes. The waitress was a backwater kid, no more than
seventeen.

"Don't you be eyeballin' Marlene," Junior said. "You
got your black meat there."

Carver thought, This is gonna be trouble. A part of him
had sensed it coming for a while. Something in his gut got
hard and cold, and ready. He ignored Junior. Took a bite
of chicken-fried steak. Chewed.

Beth was staring at him. "You catch what that asshole
said?" she whispered.

"Eat your hamburger."

"Didn't hear me, I guess," Junior said. "Ain't got goddam ears maybe, you think, B.J.?"

B.J., the thin one, took another bite of beans. "Leave
the man alone, Junior. He likes niggers, that's his business. He's a cripple. Maybe dark'ns is all he can bed."

Junior tilted back his tiny head on his thick neck and
took a long pull of beer. "Well, I don't think that's it. I
think he's bein' bad-mannered; is what."

Marlene had shrunk back against the wall near the grill.
The old man at the far end of the counter was staring into
his coffee cup. The skinny guy at the video machine pock-
eted a handful of change and loped leisurely from the restaurant. He wore rimless glasses and had greasy black hair
that curled down over his forehead. He didn't look scared.

Didn't look anything. It was time for him to leave, that was all.

Junior swiveled on his stool to face Carver directly. "Black section of town's down t'other end of the street. Got a restaurant there serves scum like you."

Carver said, "But it's not in the Michelin guide like this one."

Junior looked at B.J. "The fuck's he talkin' about tires for?"

B.J. shrugged and said, "Don't know, little bro."

Junior flexed his jaw muscles. "We don't mix the races in this part of the country, mister."

"Don't you really?"

"You and the nigger bitch head for the door," Junior said, "or you're gonna find out for sure we don't."

"I think we'll stay here for now, thanks."

B.J. stopped eating. He swallowed and cleared his throat. "Better listen, mister. Best you and the nigger get up and leave, or my baby brother here's might gonna turn mean."

Carver said, "We don't want trouble, but we plan on finishing our supper before we leave. That seems reasonable."

Junior said, "Not to us, it don't."

"Ain't' no cause for any meanness, Junior," Marlene said in a squeaky voice. "There's gonna be a problem, I'm headin' out back an' get Whiffy."

The big Harley fired up outside, then spat and roared as it accelerated down the street; the video-game player leaving. The receding rumble of the cycle's motor seemed to have a calming effect.

"Let's keep it light, please!" Marlene said.

For a moment Carver thought Marlene's plea might work. Junior and B.J. were silent. Junior was glaring at Carver with his tiny, porcine eyes. B.J. was gazing curiously at Beth. His face was narrow, his dark eyes set close together and recessed under shaggy brown eyebrows. The left side of his face didn't quite match the right, as if there'd been a tectonic shift of bone beneath the flesh.

Carver took a drink of beer and felt some of the tension

leave the air. He could breathe easier. Maybe they'd get out of here okay after all. The hostile brothers seemed to have cooled down. He took another long swallow of beer, moving very deliberately to add another measure of calm.

Beth said, "How far back in the swamp were you two dumb rednecks born?"

Fat Junior's jaw fell open. B.J. had lifted his fork, but set it back on his plate with a tiny *clink*. Marlene was edging toward the swinging doors to the kitchen. Carver casually removed his fingers from the cold beer glass and rested his hand on his cane.

Junior said, "Come again, nigger?" and got down off his stool. He was taller than Carver had thought, well over six feet, maybe pushing three hundred pounds. The tricep muscles in the backs of his thick arms flexed as he moved. He's done heavy lifting sometime in his life; there was steel beneath the fat. B.J. did nothing to restrain his huge "baby brother," and swiveled around and dropped off his stool. He was as tall as Junior.

Junior's sunburned, beefy face folded into a grin, and his tiny eyes glittered in cruel anticipation as he swaggered toward Beth. B.J. was moving toward Carver. The brothers had silently partitioned the work. Or was it recreation?

B. J. said, "Your lady shouldn't have talked that way to baby bro."

"Don't bother with the fuckin' cripple," Junior said. "Like you said, he ain't enough man to be with anything but black cunt. You just step on the worm and keep him outa my way while I learn the bitch a lesson."

"Don't underestimate the man," B.J. warned. "Some of them gimps got strong upper bodies from draggin' themselves around. 'Member that limp-legged fisherman give you a split lip last August."

"That'n was a man and this'n's a pile of shit," Junior said. He was angered even more by being reminded of whatever trouble last year's victim had given him. Great, Carver thought, just what we need, more adrenaline for Junior.

Beth hadn't budged, but now Carver saw her move her hands beneath table level. She was digging in her purse for something. A gun, he hoped; he'd left his back at the motel.

But it was only her keys. A ring of them attached to what he at first thought was a thick ballpoint pen, but was only a cylindrical piece of brushed aluminum with a dull pointed end, large enough to keep her from losing her keys in her purse.

Junior was smiling broadly and sweating hard. He smelled stale and sour, and faintly of fish. There were perspiration stains on his bib overalls. He ducked a shoulder as he got close to Beth. Reached out for her.

Carver slashed with the cane. Felt solid contact with Junior's wrist. Junior drew back his hand and rubbed the wrist, looking annoyed. He said, "Shouldn't have oughta done that." Carver knew the blow would have broken the wrist of an ordinary man, but Junior was a subspecies.

A shadow flitted in the corner of his vision. B.J. rushing him, striking like a snake.

Carver swiveled in his chair, whipped around again with the cane. It caught B.J. across the forehead and sent him reeling back. He looked astounded and enraged. Blood was flowing into his right eye from a cut at his hairline.

He said, "Why, you dirty cocksucker," and came at Carver again.

This time Carver jabbed with the cane. The tip caught B.J. in the sternum, just below the heart. Breath *whooshed!* from him as he staggered backward. He dropped to sit on the floor and began to gasp.

Carver turned to keep Junior away from Beth.

But Beth was standing and had moved toward Junior, gripping the aluminum cylinder as if it were a peg she was about to jab into the hard ground. As Junior lunged for her she dragged the sharp keys across his eyes. Wheeled so her back was to him for an instant, and struck at his genitals with the pointed end of the cylinder. All so fast it was like a choreographed and practiced dance maneuver.

Junior released his grip on her arm. He groaned, then let out a long, whistling sigh and doubled over. His forehead was pale and creased in pain. He'd just raised his

head to focus his scratched and bleeding eyes on Beth
when she screamed, startling and freezing him even if he
could have moved quickly. She hacked at his bull neck
with the edge of her hand. Carver watched, amazed. Ka-
rate bullshit.

Beth brought up her knee and caught the side of Junior's
face. Denim swished over flesh. Carver was standing, sup-
porting himself with his free hand on the table. He glanced
at B.J., who was just struggling to his feet, still gripping
his stomach. No danger there yet. Carver brought the hard
walnut cane down on top of Junior's head. The vibration
of solid contact ran up his arm as he heard the *thwack!* of
wood on flesh and bone.

Junior didn't go down, but he backed away, looking
puzzled and pressing his hand to the top of his head, as if
unfamiliar with the bother of persistently uncooperative
victims.

B.J. was standing with his lean body swaying, obviously thinking about another charge and how to handle
Carver and the cane.

A deep voice said, " 'Nuff of this shit, you *hear*!"

A broad-shouldered black man was standing near the
counter. He was holding a baseball bat in his right hand.
Marlene was cowering behind him and looking uncertain,
as if someone had threatened to sue about a fly in the soup
and she didn't know what to do.

Junior and B.J. drifted closer together and seemed to
lose interest in attacking Carver and Beth. Junior said,
"This nigger-lover started it, Whiff."

Whiffy stared at him with deep brown eyes that showed
crescents of blue-tinted white beneath the pupils. He said,
"I'd just as leave you didn't talk that way in here, Junior."

Junior said nothing, but he couldn't meet the black man's
steady stare.

B.J. said, "Things just got outa hand, is all, Whiff."

"You keep control of that brother of yours," Whiffy
said.

"No problem," B.J. said. "C'mon, little bro. We was
about finished here anyways."

Beth said, "You sure as fuck were."

Without looking at Carver and Beth, both men walked out of the restaurant. B.J. was pressing a white paper napkin to his head. Junior had one hand on his crotch. The other hand was rubbing the side of his neck where Beth had hacked at him.

Carver looked at Beth. "You okay?"

"You bet."

Whiffy said, "Don't imagine they'll forget this. A black woman an' a guy with a cane gettin' the best of 'em, you surely fuckin' with their machismo."

The old guy at the end of the counter hadn't moved. He was still staring into his coffee cup, but grinning now. Without looking up, he said, "Was the Brainard brothers started the pot boilin', Whiff."

"Figured such." Whiffy laid the bat on the counter and moved toward Carver and Beth. He was average height but thick-boned and with a compact muscularity about him. Barefoot and wearing black shorts and a gray T-shirt that said BRAVES. The flesh around his eyes was puffy, as if he'd been sleeping when Marlene had summoned him to deal with a problem in the restaurant. His ebony face was pockmarked and he had a thin black mustache neatly trimmed a half inch above his upper lip. After giving Carver an appraising stare, he smiled with even, white teeth at Beth, and with a different kind of appraisal. "Siddown, you two, an' I'll tell you the facts of life accordin' to the gospel in Dark Glades."

Carver nodded to Beth and they sat. Marlene brought two Budweisers, and another glass of ice water for Beth. A tough audience like Junior and B.J. found Whiffy worth listening to, so Carver wanted to hear what he had to say.

23

"GUESS YOU worked out my name's Whiffy," Whiffy said. "Real name's Willard Renfrow."

Carver introduced himself and Beth, and shook Whiffy's strong black hand. He noticed several fingers were crooked and had oversized knuckles, as if they were arthritic.

"They's about four hundred folks in Dark Glades," Whiffy said, after taking a hearty pull of Budweiser and flicking foam from his narrow mustache. "That includes the ones live outside the town proper. 'Bout a hundred of the citizens here are black, and they live mostly down Cypress Avenue on the east side of town. Like in a lotta towns, you'll recognize the poor, mostly black area by the ramshackle houses an' the old cars. Per capita income ain't for shit. The black families in Dark Glades are descendants of north Florida slaves moved down here after the Civil War, an' they still got a slave mentality. Civil-rights movement never really caught on in these parts, an' these last ten years it's backslid 'bout as far as it could go."

A motorcycle downshifted and roared by fast outside. The kid on the Harley? Carver said, "One thing I don't get. You're black and you own the town's main restaurant in the white section. And B.J. and his brother listened when you talked to them."

"They was listenin' to a white man."

Carver sat wondering if there might be something in the water in Dark Glades that impaired reason.

Whiffy glanced at Beth and grinned. He said, "Man don't understand. I'm good as white here for two reasons, Carver. I got money, an' I used to play pro ball. Came up from the minors to catch for the Atlanta Braves seven years ago. Went to bat a hunnerd an' fifty times, till my elbow got broke by a hard-throwin' Cardinals right-hander. Ended my career. Didn't matter; I was only hittin' .223, with thirty-five strikeouts, so the Braves were plannin' on sendin' me back down. Pitchers soon found out I had a blind spot. Couldn't hit a high, tight fastball, which is why I got tagged with the name Whiffy. That's what that right-hander threw me, an' I was too slow to get outa the way, much less hit the ball."

"You saying money and major-league status bought you respect here?"

"I'm sayin' they made me *white*. These yahoos figure a black man's inferior, so if one of us does better'n most white men in a way can't be denied, it don't tally with their thinkin'. So what they do is make him white in their minds, sort of. That way there's no breakdown of their fucked-up logic. Don't just happen here. Look around, you'll see it all the time. There's a story in baseball 'bout a manager didn't want a black player on his team. Then the man hits a triple first time at bat. Manager jumps up an' down an' yells, 'Looka that Cuban run!' "

Carver exchanged glances with Beth. She nodded, smiling sadly.

"It helps, too," Whiffy said, "that I can still swing the bat well enough to break a few skulls if I got to. And they know I'll swing it. What I'm tryin' to get across to you is that this here's a backwater town where interracial couples just ain't gonna be accepted. An' you two don't have to be sleepin' together; you just walk around together an' some of the Neanderthals around here'll be ready to lynch you both."

"Like B.J. and Junior Brainard?"

" 'Specially like them. They live in a rundown cabin

out in the swamp an' support themselves dealin' dope an'
poachin' 'gators. Get to know them two, an' you might
think the theory of evolution can work in reverse.''

Carver said, ''What about the law here?''

''That'd be Chief Ellis Morgan an' two part-time officers. He does what he can, but he's an elected official, if
you catch my meanin'.''

''He plays along with the bad guys.''

''No more'n he has to, but he plays.''

''How dangerous are the Brainard brothers?''

''They killed before, I'm sure of it. You run dope an'
you poach the way they do, murder can become part of
the game. Swamp hides bodies an' they never turn up.''
He nodded toward Beth. ''I don't mean to shock the lady,
but it's a fact.''

Carver said, ''She understands.''

Whiffy tilted his head to the side and stared at Beth.
''Where'd you learn to be such a bad-ass in a fight, Miss?''

''My husband taught me. He thought it'd be good for
me to know.''

''Husband?''

''Not me,'' Carver said.

''You two made big enough fools outa the Brainards
they ain't gonna sleep well till they make things even.
'Specially Junior, bein' fucked over like that by a woman.
So if I was you, I'd finish whatever business I had in Dark
Glades an' move along without a forwardin' address.''

Carver said, ''Sound idea.''

''Some people I run from,'' Beth said, ''some I don't.''

Whiffy shook his head. ''That martial-arts shit don't
work against a shotgun.''

''Good point,'' Carver said.

Whiffy said, ''You got sense, man. Try to talk a little
into her.''

Beth arched an eyebrow at Whiffy. ''You're still here,
and you gotta use a baseball bat from time to time.''

''I got family roots here go back to Southern Recon-
struction, honey, or I sure as hell'd be livin' in Miami
or someplace else where mosta the houses got indoor

plumbin'.'' He peered hard at Beth, then looked at Carver. "I ain't convincin' her, am I?"

"My guess is no."

"Listen here," Whiffy said, leaning so far back in his chair that Carver thought the rear legs would slide under on the smooth linoleum, "I don't know what the relationship is between you two an' don't much care. But this ain't an enlightened part of the world here. People are gonna assume the worst an' act on it, an' not necessarily accordin' to law."

Beth shot him an icy look. "We're only business associates."

"Just travelin' through, I hope."

"We plan on staying awhile," she said firmly.

"Hmm. You two at the Casa Grande?"

"How'd you know?" Beth asked.

"Only real motel close in to town."

Beth said, "Gonna be our home for a while."

Whiffy drained his beer mug, let his chair drop forward on all four legs, then stood up. "The desk clerk at the Casa, little guy name of Watts, is a good man. You get in any kinda trouble over there, it's somethin' to keep in mind."

Carver said, "Thanks, we will."

"You folks go ahead an' finish your supper now. We can warm it in the microwave if you want."

"No thanks," Beth said. "I worked up an appetite. I'd rather eat cold food than wait for hot."

Carver looked at the congealing cream gravy on his chicken-fried steak. He waved Marlene over and handed her his plate. Beth took a huge bite of her hamburger and chewed lustily. He caught a hint of onion from across the table.

Whiffy said, "Marlene, you come get me if there's any more trouble, you hear?"

"I hear, Whiffy." She disappeared into the kitchen with Carver's dinner.

Whiffy tucked his thumbs in the elastic waistband of his shorts. They sagged low. For a moment Carver thought the man might absently scratch his crotch, a major leaguer in the batter's box. Habits died hard. But he released the waistband and it snapped loudly against his stomach. He said, "You folks best not stroll around an' explore the town when you leave here."

Carver said, "We're going back to the motel."

"Good," Whiffy said. He looked at Beth and shook his head slowly. Then he walked toward the kitchen and the back exit, his hairless calf muscles bulging. His sweaty bare soles made soft ticking sounds on the linoleum with each step.

At the swinging doors behind the counter, he turned and said, "You two get back to the motel, you lock your doors."

Carver said not to worry, that was in the plan.

Beth took another bite of hamburger.

Dolly Parton began singing again as Marlene brought Carver's warmed-up supper.

AFTER LEAVING Whiffy's, Carver and Beth made one stop, at the ambitiously named but tiny Everglades Drug Emporium near the end of Cypress. The place had a plank floor, a glass-and-wood display case full of dusty bottles and discolored boxes. An old man in a yellowed white shirt and a string tie leaned near the cash register, waiting for them to decide what they wanted to buy. Next to him was a soda fountain with three stools. On a shelf behind it was one of those old green Hamilton Beach blenders used for making milkshakes in stainless-steel containers that kept them cold. Carver thought a milkshake here might taste good before they left town.

Beth bought a package of disposable razors and a tube of Colgate toothpaste. Carver picked up a bottle of Tylenol, in case the swamp humidity made his knee ache. He felt as if he might be forgetting something, but he couldn't draw it to the top of his mind.

Then they bought some magazines to read. Carver picked out *Time* and *Newsweek*. Maybe he could figure out what the hell was going on in the world. Beth chose *Vogue* and *Money*, noticed Carver smiling, and told him if he laughed she'd kick him where it hurt the most.

He didn't laugh.

That night she left the connecting door between their rooms standing open.

He realized what he should have bought at the drugstore.

24

WHEN HE awoke she was still in his bed, the white sheet pulled up to her chin, one long, golden leg protruding into the cool room and extending off the side of the mattress. Carver squinted against the brilliant morning light cascading through the crack between the drawn drapes and watched her sleep. Her eyes were closed lightly, the composition of her features calm. He remembered last night's explosion of warm flesh and desperately seeking hands and tongues. How he'd lost himself in her. She didn't seem like the same woman this morning, this long, evenly breathing image of calm.

Without opening her eyes she said, "I know you're watching me, Carver."

"How?"

"I can sense things like that. Being hunted gives that to you."

He twisted his upper body and leaned sideways, making the bedsprings squeal, and kissed her on the lips.

When he drew back, she opened her eyes and stared at him, her dark pupils sparking with morning light. "Thanks, lover."

He didn't know what to say to such a simple and sincere expression of affection and appreciation. He was a little embarrassed and tried humor. "Last night means we gotta get married." Lame.

"Can the bullshit, Carver."

"Okay, canned."

Mornings were something—mornings after certain nights before. He lay back and closed his eyes, listening. The air conditioner was humming away, but the swamp seemed very near, in the room with them. Insects screamed their perpetual frantic lament. Something grunted in the distance. A bullfrog was croaking nearby. Carver said, "Truly wild."

She misunderstood, reaching a hand out from beneath the sheet and touching his arm. "No, you were gentle."

He looked at her. "Last night was gentle?"

"Comparatively speaking."

Carver thought about Roberto Gomez and liked him even less.

Beth slid both hands behind her head and lay staring up at the ceiling. "I had an uncle used to do a lotta fishing, Carver. He'd tell me that sometimes life was like a lake."

"Deep," Carver said.

She glanced over at him to see if he was trying to be funny again. He wasn't sure himself. She said, "You fish in the Midwest and you learn something. In the spring, when the lakes thaw and warm up from the sun, the water in the bottom, below the frost line, has stayed warmer all winter and warms up even faster than the top half of the lake. The fire of summer's stayed alive in it all those cold months. When it gets warm enough, it rises and the cooler water sinks. An inversion's the technical term. The lake turns, as they say; bottom water on top, top water on the bottom, where it stays cooler all summer. That's when the season's really changed and the fishing gets good in the spring, soon as the lake turns. Well, sometimes people's lives turn that same way. A kinda change brought on by a different season."

"I'm not sure about that," Carver said. "People aren't lakes."

"You don't know till you fish."

"People have control." Then why did he feel guilty

about betraying Edwina? And as worried as a high school kid after his first sexual experience?

She said, "I didn't have control last night. You didn't, either."

"I wouldn't argue."

"Bet you wouldn't."

He shifted his weight on the bed. His lower leg accidentally touched hers. He left it there.

"Incidentally," she said, "when Adam was born I had a tubal ligation; no way I can get pregnant again."

Hmm. He scooted over to her. Kissed her on the lips, hard this time, using his tongue.

At first she didn't respond. Then her long, lithe arms unwound from behind her head and wrapped around him. He heard the sheet rustling as she worked it off her body. She moaned and pressed the firm, eager length of herself against him. He lost control again.

After the initial rush of passion they made love very deliberately, savoring each other. When they were finished, Beth lay with her head resting sideways on Carver's bare chest, as if listening to his heart. Her eyes were blank with passion spent. He'd given her the temporary escape she'd sought.

After a while she raised her face to his and kissed him, then swiveled her supple, dark body and stood up. Her thinness made her seem very tall. Even taller as she raised her arms and arched her back to stretch. She stood that way for a moment, arms out wide and hands dangling limply, a casual crucifixion.

She smiled down at him, then she bent at the waist, picked up her silk panties, and moved toward her room. As she walked away nude in the bright morning light, her lean, taut body writhed like dark flame.

Carver, breathless, said, "My God!"

She glanced back. "Huh?"

"Nothing." He grinned at her.

She closed the connecting door, and five minutes later he heard her shower running.

Carver reached for his watch on the nightstand and angled it so its dial didn't reflect light. Nine-thirty.

He sat up on the edge of the bed and pulled the phone to him. He couldn't call Edwina at home; it was possible her line had been tapped by Gomez, or maybe even Mc-Gregor, trying to keep tabs on him. He direct-dialed the Quill Realty number.

Quill's honey-voiced receptionist said Miss Talbot was in, asked who was calling, then told him just a minute and put him on hold. Muzak played, a neutered Rolling Stones number from the sixties. Moss had gathered.

The music stopped and Edwina's voice said, "Fred?"

She sounded like a stranger. "Fred," Carver confirmed.

"Where are you?"

"Can't say."

"Sure, I forgot." Her voice was disinterested.

"I called to make sure you were all right."

"You're the one supposed to be in danger," she said.

"Yeah, that's true."

"Fred?"

"Why do you keep saying that? Like you're not sure it's me?"

"I told Jack Lester I'd take the position in Hawaii, Fred."

Just like that. Over the phone. He didn't feel guilty now. He felt injured deep inside, even though he'd expected this. Even, he knew, secretly hoped for it.

"Fred?"

"Christ stop saying that!"

"Saying what?"

"My name."

"I'm sorry. But you understand my decision, don't you?"

"I understand." And he did, though not all of it. Maybe nobody ever really understood all of something like this.

"Gonna come with me?" she asked.

He didn't hesitate. They both knew the answer. "No, I can't."

"Why not?"

"A list of reasons. When do you leave?"

"Two weeks," she said.

"I'll see you before then."

"When?"

"I don't know for sure."

"Okay, Fred."

He could think of nothing to say. He had nothing for this woman he'd lived with and eaten with and slept with and held in the night.

Nothing to say to her.

There was a silence that lasted light-years before she said softly, " 'Bye."

He told her good-bye and hung up.

The swamp was in the room now, in his head. Screaming and thrumming and sucking and croaking.

Primal and deadly.

Alive and frightening.

He closed his fingers around his cane propped against the nightstand. Slowly raised it and touched its tip to the wall, as if to reassure himself there was a barrier between him and what was wild and incomprehensible in the outside world.

A full minute passed before he broke contact with the solid wall and lowered the cane.

He leaned back on the bed and gazed up at the ceiling, where Beth had been staring, and he trembled with a chill.

Lakes turning.

25

CARVER SAT up in the bed when he heard the crunch of tires on gravel stop right outside the door. He felt his bare back stick to the headboard above his wadded pillow. Reaching his cane, he stood up and hobbled to the window. He peered out through the crack between the drawn drapes, narrowing his eyes against the morning glare.

A dusty white Ford with red and blue roof-bar lights was parked next to the Olds. It had a thick, bent antenna jutting from a rear fender. A blue and gold shield on the door, with what looked like a decal of an alligator above it, said DARK GLADES POLICE. Above the alligator, black letters spelled out CHIEF. A man with a Smokey hat sat behind the steering wheel. His face was in shadow, but he was obviously staring out the windshield at Carver.

Carver didn't pull away from the window. He watched as a tall, well-built man in a blue uniform climbed out of the car and nonchalantly slammed the door. A holstered revolver, a nightstick, and handcuffs dangled from his thick black belt, along with a square, black walkie-talkie. All that paraphernalia made him walk with a lazy swagger, arms floating out to the side to keep them from bumping equipment. He was young and had a handsome, angular face. A friendly face. He smiled at Carver as he passed from sight. His knock on the door was soft but insistent. The foreplay of the law.

Carver limped to the door and opened it.

The man was still smiling amiably. He looked more like a college football hero than a backwater town police chief. A broad-shouldered wide receiver who could run and block and would be hard to bring down.

"I'm Chief of Police Ellis Morgan," the man said.

Carver nodded. "Fred Carver."

"I know." Morgan made a face and glanced in the direction of the fierce morning sun angling fire in over the treetops. "Can I come in where it's cool, Mr. Carver?"

"Sure, sorry." Carver stepped back and to the side. Morgan eased past him, glancing at the cane, no surprise or pity in his eyes. He removed his Smokey hat and let spring a shock of thick black hair. hatless he looked even younger, no more than twenty-five.

"Feels good in here," he said, dabbing at his forehead with a blue shirt sleeve. His friendly blue eyes did a turn around the room and didn't flicker when they took in the bed, which had obviously been slept in by two. He said, "Came by to talk about the trouble happened in Whiffy's yesterday evening."

"It's over, I hope," Carver said.

Morgan let out breath in a way that made little popping sounds between his pursed lips. "Nope, not likely. The Brainards aren't the type to let something like what happened go by. I mean, your lady friend, black woman at that, was whipping ass on big Junior when Whiffy broke it up. Old Farnham was watching from where he sat at the counter, said lucky for the Brainards Whiffy came in when he did, or they'd have been royally stomped." He grinned. "That the way it went?"

"That's how it might have gone," Carver said.

"The lady said her husband taught her to fight tough like that. Martial-arts stuff. And you're not her husband?"

"I'm a friend."

The blue eyes darted to the bed and back. "Now and then we get tourists stay here, Mr. Carver. For the fishing or to take airboat rides or some such. But I tell you, you don't strike me as the fisherman type.''

"How about airboats?''

"Around here, Mr. Carver, airboats are mostly used to poach 'gator or smuggle drugs. You don't want me to think you might be *that* type.''

Carver said, "I'm glad I'm not wearing my alligator shoes.''

Morgan leaned back with his buttocks against the edge of the dresser and crossed his arms, still with his amiable country smile. Maybe he slept wearing that expression. "I gotta be impressed, a guy puts up here at the motel, drops by Whiffy's for supper with his lady, then the two of them are well on their way to whaling bejesus outa the town's leading muscle. Go ahead and eat their supper after the commotion dies down. I mean, ordinary folks just don't behave such a way.''

Carver said, "Sure came as a surprise to B.J. and Junior.''

"Lots in life surprises them boys.'' Morgan idly twirled his hat in both hands by its stiff brim. "Mr. Carver, you're some rough man, even though you walk with a cane.''

"Cane can be a potent weapon.''

" 'Pears that's true. And you look in fine physical shape other than the bum leg. How'd you pick it up, car accident?''

"I was hit by something,'' Carver said. He saw that the chief wanted to find out more but had decided not to ask.

Morgan said instead, "What kinda work you in?''

Carver figured it was wise not to underestimate the man, young and backwater or not. "I'm a private investigator from up north.''

"North?''

"Central Florida.''

"On a case?''

"Not exactly. Just here with my friend. She's a Florida State student and she's received some threats from the people where she lives. Because I stay there overnight sometimes. It's a condo where the neighbors are mostly from Southern states and don't think highly of interracial love.''

"Love, is it?"

"Maybe. You're getting awful personal, Chief.''

"Well, I don't give a damn what you two are to each other. None of my business. I'm trying to save you and the lady some trouble, Mr. Carver. You see, compared to here in Dark Glades, the neighbors at the condo up north might seem like the NAACP.''

"Whiffy led me to believe that.''

"He's right. Whiffy's a good man to listen to. Lived a lotta his life out away from here. Played baseball in the minor leagues, then did a brief stint with the Atlanta Braves. Poor guy couldn't hit the high hard one.''

"He told me,'' Carver said. "He was a catcher.''

"Yeah, tell that looking at his hands.'' Morgan stood up straight and his expression changed. He was smiling more warmly. "Morning, ma'am.''

Standing in the doorway to her room, Beth smiled and returned his good morning. She was wearing her jeans and a khaki shirt that had oversized pockets with flaps over her breasts. Her hair was still glistening with water from her shower, and she was barefoot.

Carver looked at her and said, "This is Police Chief Ellis Morgan.''

She came the rest of the way into the room. "I overheard while I was getting dressed.'' She sat down on the bed and crossed her legs. Her presence seemed to make Morgan nervous. He was young, all right, and hadn't seen many women of any color with Beth's high voltage.

Morgan made himself look into her eyes. Brave man. He said, "You from Del Moray like Mr. Carver?''

Carver realized Morgan had run a make on his license number, gotten his address.

"No,'' Beth said, "I live farther south. I go to school.''

"Having trouble where you live, I understand.''

Beth said, "Yes, I am. That's why we wanted to get away for a while.''

Morgan said, "I wish I could say you came to the right

spot. Wish I could advise you to stay." He looked at Carver. "Instead I gotta advise you to leave."

Beth's voice was incredulous. "You're running us out of town?"

Morgan laughed. "Lord, no. I wouldn't do that even if I could. Anyway, I admire what you did last night. Thing is, Junior and B.J. are into illegal drugs. Maybe Carver here knows how nasty that game can be, or maybe he don't. But I'm telling you it can be rough. And the people in it value their reputations for toughness. Last night you shredded Junior's bad-boy image, and he's gotta get it back. I mean, just gotta! Even if he wasn't a stupid, vengeful bastard, it'd be good business for him. Necessary business. So the two of you stay around Dark Glades, you can just about count on more trouble."

Beth said, "Are you offering us protection if we don't leave?"

"Sure. But I gotta be honest, I can't protect you 'round the clock from the Brainards. Only me and two officers on the force. We got two patrol cars, and one's running about half the time. The city budget kinda limits what I can do for you."

"Go talk to the Brainards," Beth suggested. "Scare them into thinking of other matters."

"Gotta talk gorilla to get through to them boys. Not real advanced gorilla, at that. Running drugs, poaching 'gators, whipping ass—that's what their lives are about. You snatched a third of that away by making them into fools in Whiffy's. Ain't a big place, Dark Glades, and talk gets passed around like a common cold, only quicker."

Carver said, "How big is the drug trade around here?"

Morgan shrugged. "Shit, folks in these parts grow the stuff like it was dandelions. And what they don't grow they buy and pass on for profit. Not many other ways to make money in a place like this. Tell you the truth, I'd suspect that was why you were in town, as part of some kinda drug deal. Only if that was so, you probably wouldn't've mixed it up with the Brainards; they'd have been in on the deal or known about it." He edged toward the door, putting on his hat and fastening the strap beneath his chin.

He smiled widely at them. "I just wanted to meet you two after what you did last night. Wanted to let you know how things stood in Dark Glades. We ain't what you'd call a progressive city, I'm afraid. Around here, affirmative action means a lynching."

Carver said, "Whiffy's done okay."

"Well, Whiffy, he's another story."

"He's black."

"Not exactly," the chief said. "Not in what you'd call the Dark Glades sense. He's been around, Whiffy has. To the big leagues and the big cities. Makes him sort of cosmopolitan. Whiffy's different."

Beth stood up, looking beautifully angry. "We're all different, Chief Morgan. Don't you watch 'Geraldo'?"

"So you are," Morgan said. His smile looked as if it might slip off his face and shatter at his feet like crystal. "Didn't mean to insult you, ma'am." He sounded genuinely sorry.

Beth didn't answer.

At the door he turned and said, "Wish you folks'd be sensible and leave. Avoid real trouble."

Carver said, "We'll think about it. Thanks for the advice, Chief."

"Do try to talk some sense into the lady." He extended two fingers, as in a Cub Scout salute, and tapped the brim of his hat. "Been a pleasure."

He shut the door behind him, but not before a couple of flies had found their way in.

Carver stood with both hands folded over the crook of his cane. He listened to Morgan's car start, then the gravelly crunch of tires as it backed out of its parking slot. When it got straightened out and accelerated, there was a deeper rattle of gravel.

The flies that had been let in circled and buzzed against the light filtering through the drapes. They sounded desperate. Carver looked down at Beth, still perched on the edge of the bed with her legs crossed. He said, "We better talk about this."

Beth said, "Sure. Talk's cheap."

"Sometimes life is, too."

"I can only run from one thing at a time, Carver. You think these pissant redneck drug dealers scare me?"

My, *my.* "I dunno. They scare me."

She grinned and said, "Yeah, but only up to a point."

He looked at his new lover, the marked-for-murder wife of the drug kingpin. Not Edwina, but a woman who was in many ways still a stranger. He felt a cold and echoing emptiness.

Yet, in a stronger sense, Beth was anything *but* a stranger. Momentum had them. They were moving toward each other in a vortex of new and unknown passion, the age-old endless discovery. It was a whirlpool neither could resist, and neither wanted to escape.

26

BY THE time the fried eggs and bacon arrived at their table at Whiffy's, Beth was no longer misty-eyed. Before they'd left the motel, she'd called again to check on Adam and had a lengthy, tearful phone conversation with Melanie. Carver figured there was a time limit on keeping mother and child separated. He wasn't sure how long that might be.

Marlene the waitress gave them each a shy grin as she set the plates before them. She glanced with unabashed awe at Beth, then told them to signal when they wanted more coffee. She returned to the sizzling grill behind the counter.

There were about a dozen customers in Whiffy's, mostly rough-looking men. Just three women, one of them very old and almost bald. No sign of Whiffy this morning. Maybe he only appeared when there was trouble, when Marlene drew him like a gun. Occasionally, one of the men would look over at Carver and Beth, features set in barely disguised hostility. The women were less reserved in letting their faces show their curiosity and disapproval. Carver experienced what Beth must have felt all her life in places like this. He wondered how a person learned to live with it and not explode.

The scent of the eggs and bacon wafted up to him, spur-

ring his appetite. Beth was pouring cream in her coffee.
She seemed calm now, completely over her phone call.
And seemingly unconcerned about the attitude of Whiffy's
clientele. It was, after all, what she'd expected.

He picked up his fork and began to eat.

The eggs were greasy but good. Biscuits were terrific.
Coffee strong, the way Carver liked it. He could see why
Whiffy's had no serious competition in Dark Glades.

When they were finished eating and on their second
cups of coffee, Carver said, "Sure you wanna stay here?
It doesn't make much sense to me."

"Yes it does," Beth said. "You understand."

"You're running for your life," Carver reminded her.

She sipped her coffee and considered. Above her, one
of the ceiling fans ticked like a metronome as its wide
blades rotated. "Might be this kinda trouble wherever we
go."

"Not in a big city. We could lose ourselves in Miami.
Or maybe the Tampa area."

"You kidding, Carver? Those are the places Roberto
operates heaviest and has the most connections. You were
the one came up with the idea of going to the boondocks,
and it was a good one."

"That was before we knew what kinda place this was.
Before we met Junior and B.J. Brainard."

Beth stared at him with something like pleading in her
dark eyes. "Carver, you gotta understand, I just can't run
from people like Junior and B.J.; I made it the basis of
my whole life, not running from them and their kind."

"You mean you joined them instead?"

She sat back and looked as if he'd kicked her in the
stomach.

He reached for his cup, then set it back down without
having raised it more than an inch. "Damn it, I didn't
mean it like that, Beth! You know it."

She gave him a neutral look that shielded all emotion.
How often had she worn that mask in Gomez's presence?
"Life fucks us over, all of us."

"True enough. Really, I wasn't being judgmental."

"Besides, in the beginning Roberto wasn't the way he is now."

"I believe you, but if you don't mind, I'll go ahead and be judgmental about Roberto."

"The money did it to him, Carver. You realize what it means to have that much money? You wouldn't believe how *much* money, green and endless. For Roberto, there's always a limitless supply. He expects to have everything he wants. There isn't anything he can't afford, and can't have on his terms."

"You," Carver pointed out.

"Yeah, that's right. But I'm the exception to the rule. That's why he has to try to kill me." She finished her coffee and set the cup down hard in its saucer. "The Brainards aren't gonna be a problem, trust me. They'll slink back into the swamp where they belong, and do whatever it is they do. I've seen men like that. There isn't any substance to them."

"Chief Morgan knows them, and he thinks they're substantive enough to squeeze triggers."

She laughed softly. "Roberto makes them look tame. Roberto's enemies make them look like kittens." She sounded as if she were bragging about Gomez. Carver didn't like that.

He buttered and ate his last biscuit, then summoned Marlene and paid the check. Left a two-dollar tip. Marlene acted as if it were twenty dollars. Apparently not much of the drug money changing hands in and around Dark Glades found its way to waitresses. There was no democracy in crime.

Chief Morgan was walking into Whiffy's as Carver and Beth were leaving. He showed his young Gary Cooper smile and nodded to them as he ambled over to a corner table. Marlene had seen him and was already on the way with a cup of coffee.

The sun and humidity were teaming up tough again today. Carver figured if he'd had creases in his pants, they would have disappeared by the time he and Beth reached the car.

They were driving back to the motel over a rutted,

slightly elevated dirt road when a rumbling sound, then motion in the rearview mirror, caught Carver's attention.

A four-wheel-drive Chevy Blazer with huge knobbed tires crawled up from the swamp onto the road and fell in behind the Olds. It was dented and rusty, painted in dull green and brown camouflage.

Carver studied it in the mirror. Suddenly it grew, as it roared up close to the Olds's rear bumper. No mistaking who was in the Blazer now: B.J. Brainard was driving; the massive shape beside him was baby brother Junior.

Beth had turned and was staring back at them. She seemed afraid, but mostly she looked angry. "Those assholes!" she said, as if they were merely messing up the morning and weren't in the least homicidal.

Carver held the Olds's speed at a steady twenty miles per hour, letting the Blazer eat dust from the dry road. "Morgan warned us," he said, "just didn't warn us how soon."

The Blazer fell back about a hundred feet, so B.J. could see more clearly through the thick haze. It held that distance, a tall and outsize cariacture of a truck, its huge tires beating at the road.

Turned in her seat, Beth watched it out the back window until Carver braked the Olds and steered into the Casa Grande's parking lot.

The Blazer followed and parked nose-out at the opposite side of the lot. It sat with engine idling as Carver and Beth climbed out of the Olds and went into Carver's room. The irregular, deep beat of its motor suggested custom work and plenty of power.

There was only one other car on the lot, a pale blue Plymouth, the kind rental companies used, parked at the far end of the motel. No one in sight.

The rumbling low thunder of the Blazer's engine could be heard even inside the room with the door shut. Beth, still looking more irritated than afraid, said, "What now?"

"Up to them," Carver said. "That's what I don't like about staying around Dark Glades."

Beth shot him a dark and furious glance. "Gonna give me the old I-told-you-so shit, Carver?"

The phone rang before he had a chance to tell her that was what he was going to do.

When Carver picked up the receiver, Watts said, "I happened to glance out the office window, Mr. Carver. Saw the Brainard brothers' truck out on the lot. Them two boys are sittin' in it watchin' your room."

"Thanks, Watts, we know they're there."

"Want I should phone Chief Morgan?"

"Not yet," Carver said. "Call him if they come inside."

"Will do." Watts hung up.

Carver limped to the dresser and pulled the Colt automatic out from beneath his folded shirts, then got the loaded clip out from under a pair of Jockey shorts and slid it in. Tapped it tight. He worked the handgun's mechanism to jack a round into the chamber. The solid clicking of precision steel was comforting.

Beth was looking over his shoulder, standing so close he could feel her breath on his neck and pick up the faint scent of her morning coffee. She said, "I got one of those in my room. Want me to get it?"

"Jockey shorts?"

"Don't be a wise-ass at a time like this."

He said, "No better time. Leave your gun where it is for now."

She said, "You forget who hired whom?"

He liked that *whom*, but he didn't answer her. She made no move to go to her room and get the gun he hadn't known about. If the Brainards climbed down out of their truck and walked toward them, he'd send her for more firepower. Until then, why increase the odds on an accidental exchange of shots?

As if responding to what he was thinking, the Blazer's engine fell silent. The passenger-side door swung open and Junior hopped to the ground. The truck's heightened suspension and oversized tires created quite a drop, and his huge stomach jiggled when his boots hit gravel. He reached back into the Blazer and pulled out a shotgun. The other door opened, and B.J. sprang to the ground, light and lean as a jungle cat. He was carrying a handgun, had a large sheath knife attached to his belt, and was wearing some kind of round gray fur cap despite the heat. Looked like Davy Crockett gone bad. They were some pair, the Brainards.

The brothers glanced at each other. Junior grinned. They moved out away from the Blazer and walked toward Carver's room, keeping distance between them.

Carver looked at Beth and said, ''Really know how to use that gun?''

She looked scared now, but she nodded.

''Go get it. Don't use it unless I tell you.''

She didn't answer, but moved quickly and gracefully to the connecting door, opened it, and disappeared into her room.

Carver parted the drapes slightly wider and peered back out the window.

The Brainards had stopped and were standing in the sun-cooked parking lot, about fifty feet from the door to Carver's room. They knew he was watching. Junior, still grinning, winked at him. There was nasty anticipation smeared all over his fat face.

Half a minute passed and no one moved. Possibly the purpose of the Brainards' visit was to terrorize and not to act. Cats and mice at play. Cats, anyway.

Carver thought, Fuck this. Holding the Colt at his side, its safety off, he went to the door and opened it. Stepped outside.

Neither of the Brainards seemed surprised.

Junior said, ''Mornin', asshole.''

Carver didn't answer.

B.J. said, ''Get it in your mind, Carver, we can open fire on you here and you're a dead soldier. No way you can drop both of us afore we kill you.''

Carver said, ''Junior'll be my pick. He's a nice wide target.''

Junior stopped grinning. Sensitive about his weight. He said, ''Thing to remember about us, Carver, is we just don't give a fuck. Honestly don't. That's why we don't scare.''

Carver said, "Times like this, I feel exactly the same way, so don't stand there wasting my time with bullshit."

Junior and B.J. exchanged glances. Junior said, "Thinks he's a tough asshole 'steada just an asshole."

B.J. said, "Well, dead's dead. He wants his tombstone to say he was tough, that's okay."

Junior spread his feet wide and angled his body, in position to raise the shotgun to his shoulder. "You ready, B.J.?"

Carver figured they were bluffing, but he couldn't deny the terror that spread through him. He centered his weight between his good leg and his cane. Tightened his finger on the Colt's trigger.

Behind him, Beth's voice said, "We're sure as fuck ready."

Junior's little pig eyes actually widened. His body tensed and he drifted around to face Carver square. B.J. looked confused, letting his revolver dangle loose at his side.

Beth moved up to stand beside Carver. She was holding an Uzi submachine gun in a way that left no doubt she knew how to use it. The resolve in her eyes left no doubt that she would.

Junior and B.J. unconsciously backed away a few steps. They knew there was enough firepower in Beth's hands to kill them ten times over within seconds.

Carver smiled.

B.J. stared at him and said, "What the fuck is she, some kinda African female mercenary?"

Junior, looking enraged now and showing some guts, said, "That what you are, nigger?"

"Not a mercenary," Beth told him, "just a psychotic killer." She raised the Uzi.

The Brainard brothers' mouths fell open. They couldn't know if she was serious. Couldn't know her finger wouldn't twitch on the trigger even if she *wasn't* serious. As B.J. had pointed out, dead was dead.

Neither brother turned around. Still facing Carver and Beth, they backed slowly toward the Blazer. Every few steps, Junior whipped his head around on his thick neck to make sure they were moving in a straight line, shortest distance between two points. Then his glittering pinpoint eyes fixed again on Beth.

When they reached the Blazer, Junior yanked open the door and scrambled inside, anxious to get metal between himself and submachine gun bullets. Never averting his intense and angry stare, B.J. raised himself up behind the steering wheel slowly, wary and controlled.

The Blazer's starter ground and the engine kicked over. The truck lurched as B.J. shoved it into gear.

B.J. and Junior were still watching Beth as the Blazer rolled on its wide, knobbed tires toward the driveway. When the hood was aimed at the road, Junior stuck his head out the window and yelled, "We'll be back, bitch!"

The Blazer's engine howled and its tires threw gravel and blue-black smoke as it tore out of the lot and the line of fire.

Beth waved the Uzi and snarled, "Yellow shit bastards!"

Carver said, "Calm down." Trying to calm down himself. His stomach was tight, and the taste of metal lay thick on the edges of his tongue. Death had been close.

"He needs to learn not to call people 'nigger,' " Beth said.

Carver looked down at the Uzi. "You've got what it takes to teach him."

She exhaled loudly in that way of hers, puffing out her cheeks. "Roberto's got these things laying around like ashtrays. Thought I might as well bring one with me when I left."

Carver said, "It loaded?"

"Damn right, it's loaded. And I was within a half-inch of using it."

Terrific, Carver thought. "You sure you're not some kinda African mercenary?"

She smiled.

He said, "Let's go inside outa this heat. I need to make a phone call."

DESOTO WAS at his desk. When the lieutenant picked up his phone in Orlando, Carver could hear Latin music in the background. A merengue, heavy on the guitars. After Carver identified himself, the music faded.

"You okay, *amigo*?"

Carver said he was.

"And the Gomez woman?"

"Okay too."

"Hmm."

"Anything I oughta know on that end?" Carver asked.

Desoto said, "I got word our friend McGregor's trying very hard to find you."

"He would be."

"He's also got some kinda semi-secret operation going in Del Moray. Seems to think there's gonna be a major drug drop there."

"*Semi*-secret?"

"Yeah, that DEA guy, Dan Strait, found out about it. He's cut himself in. Too many people know what's happening for it to work, you ask me. All those people, somebody's bound to tip the drug runners. They have connections all through the Florida police. Even the DEA."

"Comforting thought."

"For them."

Carver said, "Beth and I are getting a rough time from two brothers here who're said to be in the drug trade. B.J. and Junior Brainard. Ever hear of them?"

"You forget I don't know where you are, *amigo*."

"Okay, a little town called Dark Glades, in the Everglades. But if anybody asks you, there is no such place. You might really think that if you were here with us."

"All right. But even if I never heard of Park Glades—"

"*Dark* Glades."

"Okay—I could check with the law there and see what's the deal with these brothers."

"The law's a guy named Morgan and a two-man police force. It's a small town."

"Maybe the DEA has got something on the Brainard brothers. But if I check with them, they'll know something's up in Dark Glades. They haven't stopped thinking about you and Mrs. Gomez, my friend."

"What about *Mister* Gomez?"

"I understand Roberto's disappeared. But that's not unusual; he's dropped from sight plenty of times. But this time would it have to do with a drug drop in or near Del Moray?"

"Might."

"Then McGregor's not wasting his time?"

"Not entirely. Unless he goes about things the wrong way."

"The weasely bastard has a way of doing things the wrong way and still coming out on top."

"So far, anyway. Maybe he'll nail Gomez. And if he doesn't, Strait's got a chance."

A long silence buzzed and crackled on the line. "You're the one put McGregor onto the drug drop, aren't you? So he's got a shot to nail Gomez before he can catch up with your client."

"I'm a taxpayer," Carver said. "Why shouldn't McGregor work for me?"

"If he gets Gomez for keeps, he might work for you as mayor."

"A risk, but McGregor running for mayor is better than Gomez running free."

"Agreed, but it's a close call."

"Does Gomez have any drug dealings in the swampland?"

"Anywhere in Florida, he's maybe got his hand in. Drug types are thick with each other until money causes a falling-out and bullets start to zip. You want me to check with the DEA on these Brainard brothers?"

Carver thought about it, then said, "No, I think I better take on only one monster at a time."

"Same monster, *amigo,* just a different head."

"Greek mythology?"

"American reality."

Carver gave Desoto the Casa Grande's phone number, but told him he probably wouldn't be in Dark Glades much longer.

Beth stared at him questioningly as he said this.

As Carver hung up the phone, they both turned toward the rubber-on-gravel growl of an approaching vehicle.

The Brainards' Blazer coming back?

Carver limped to the window and looked outside.

Chief Morgan was climbing out of his dusty white patrol car, hitching up his pants.

Carver wasn't surprised. Watts had seen the guns.

27

As CHIEF MORGAN approached, Carver limped to the door and opened it. Sun glinted off the patrol car's windshield. Warm outside air rolled in around Carver. The fetid stench of the swamp enveloped him, and for an instant he sensed in a primitive part of his brain the remorseless saga of survival being played out in the green arena of the Everglades.

The chief politely removed his Smokey hat again as he slid past Carver into the room; he had about him an odd courtliness that didn't suit his occupation. He nodded to Beth, holding his hat flat against his genitalia, as if she might try to kick him there. Today he had on high black leather boots, and they creaked like rocking-chair runners with each step.

He smiled at Carver and said, "More trouble with the Brainard brothers, huh?"

"They were here," Carver said, "made some threats."

"With weapons, way I understand."

"That's right."

Morgan cocked his head to the side and looked at Beth. Amusement might have flickered in his guileless blue eyes. "Brainards leave because they were outgunned?"

Beth said, "You'd have to ask them why."

"Wouldn't be much point," the chief said. "Like there

don't seem much point in asking you two. I'll talk to 'em, though. They'll most likely say they was never here, that you're lying about this morning. No way to prove otherwise, I'm afraid. It'd be senseless to ask a witness to step forward and speak against the Brainard brothers unless they were sure to be put away for a lotta years. Brainards know that, too. They count on it.'' He looked wearily at Carver. "In light of what happened here, I thought I better come over and see if I could convince you this time to leave Dark Glades. I mean, I don't wanna be the one has to clean you off the ground, and my perception is events are heading that way.''

Carver said, "We'll try to see they don't get there."

"Naturally," Morgan said. "Even so, I figure I better know more about you and the lady, Mr. Carver. So I'll be honest with you; I'm gonna go back to my office and get on the phone and the fax machine. Do some checking up on you two. I regret to say I don't think you been completely honest with me. If I don't like what I hear, I'm gonna get more insistent that you leave."

Beth stood up straighter. "And if we refuse to leave?"

"Don't get all tight in the jaw," Morgan told her. "I'm trying not to act like Marshal Dillon 'Gunsmoke' reruns, 'cause I know this is real life. But if you refuse to leave, I might have to look into the matter of an automatic weapon being brandished about."

Beth said, "I'm sure there are lots of automatic weapons in the area."

The chief said, "Yeah, that's sorta my point. I don't want this thing to escalate."

Carver said, "Sounds like you're twisting our arms, Chief."

"Guess I am, because I know the Brainards better'n you do. You could be walking around with Stinger missiles and it wouldn't help against them, 'cause they either got guided missiles of their own, or they'll shoot you in the back from ambush casual, as if you was jackrabbits in season."

Beth said, "We're not rabbits."

"So I understand." He gave his hat a few twirls between nimble fingers. "All I'm asking is you reconsider staying here and courting trouble. I believe that's reasonable.''

"It is," Carver agreed, ignoring the look Beth aimed at him.

"So talk to the lady," Morgan urged. "Some women got too much fire in their blood, and I'm afraid she's one of 'em."

Carver said, "Don't worry, we'll talk."

Morgan shook his head. "Hard not to worry, way the last couple days have gone." A helicopter-size mosquito that had entered with him circled down on the back of the hand holding the hat. Morgan slapped at it with his other hand but missed. "Well, I done all I can. Police number's there in the front of the phone book if the Brainards come back." He lowered the hat to his side and ambled to the door. "No offense, but I hope I don't hear from you. Hope I don't see either of you again."

Beth smiled and said, "No offense taken, Chief."

Morgan gave her a reciprocal smile and a final, appraising stare. Nodding good-bye to Carver, he opened the door. He plunked his hat square on his head as he walked out, swinging his arms wide.

As soon as the door closed, Carver said, "We're leaving."

Beth shook her head. "I don't see it that way."

"Not because of the Brainard brothers," he told her, "because of Chief Morgan. He'll do what he said, go to his office and start checking on me. He'll probably consult the Del Moray police."

"So what? We—"

She bit off her words, suddenly aware of what Carver was thinking.

"If the police, or even the DEA, find out where we are, it's possible Roberto'll soon know. There are certain lines of communication between the law and big-time drug dealers. You told me yourself how the law was riddled with bent bureaucrats."

Beth said, "Yeah, Roberto can find out from the cops where Chief Morgan's information request came from. And fast. He has informers in places that'd surprise you."

"He can't shock me," Carver said. "I've met his wife."

"*Former* wife," Beth corrected. "That's how I try to think of myself, anyway, even if it's not quite true yet."

Carver leaned on his cane and touched her shoulder. Felt the physical energy of passion flow into him. "I think of you that way, too."

"How long you figure it'd take Roberto go get here, once he finds out the police chief of Dark Glades requested information about us?"

"He might be here by this time tomorrow," Carver said. "To play it safe, we need to leave before nightfall."

"So let's pack," Beth said. "Get away from here soon as we can." She was plainly apprehensive now, taking Roberto Gomez much more seriously than she did the simple brute threat of the Brainards.

Carver thought getting away that soon was a good idea. He got his suitcase and slung it onto the bed. Beth disappeared into her room to get busy. As he emptied the dresser drawers, he could hear her moving around on the other side of the wall. The big mosquito that had assaulted Chief Morgan made a pass at him. He swatted at it, knocking it to the floor, stepped on it. Simple. Maybe things were starting to break the right way, the planets swinging into line, luck changing and odds brightening. Could be.

Within a half hour they had their clothes stuffed in their suitcases. Carver told Beth to stay inside while he walked over to the office to return the keys and tell Watts they were leaving earlier than planned. He left her standing between the two suitcases near the door.

But instead of going to the motel office, he stood in the stifling heat and then limped back into the room, remembering the large sheath knife on B.J. Brainard's belt.

Beth asked him what was wrong, sounding worried, and he motioned for her to look out the window at the car while he used the phone to call for a tow truck from Dark Glades.

All four of the Olds's tires were flat. They'd been slashed dozens of times with a wide-bladed knife that someone had wielded with the enthusiasm of Jack the Ripper.

Carver and Beth would have to leave Dark Glades tonight or tomorrow, or whenever new tires were available for the Olds.

Beth turned away from the window. "The Brainless brothers!" she said venomously.

Carver said, "They're not very innovative, but you almost have to admire their persistence."

"*You* admire them," Beth said. She strode angrily back to her room.

Too much fire.

| 28 |

Within an hour a dusty red tow truck with Murray's Garage lettered on its door, and a thick chain clanging musically against its stubby steel boom, rumbled into the Casa Grande parking lot. It was old and its left front fender was missing.

Carver and Beth watched out the window as it positioned itself behind the Olds. The truck jerked back and forth, its tires tossing gravel. The racket of its motor caused an explosion of birds to fan up and out darkly from the edge of the swamp.

The tow truck's door opened and a short, husky man in grease-stained gray coveralls leaped from the cab. He stood for a moment swaying, his chest puffed out and his hands floating at his sides, like a cocky astronaut who'd just emerged from a spaceship into different gravity. Then he examined the stub of a cigar jutting from his mouth to make sure he hadn't bitten into it during the impact of his drop to the ground.

Carver limped outside and said hello to him. Saw that he was about fifty and had a chubby, ruddy face that was so grease-stained it made him resemble an Indian warrior painted and ready to fight. A miniature Crazy Horse, lost in time.

The little guy even smelled like oil. Gnats swarmed

around him, but he didn't seem to notice. The name tag sewn crookedly onto his coveralls said his name was Jack Murray.

He said, "You the guy what called? A Mr. Carver?"

Carver said he was.

"Jack Murray," said the stocky little man. He propped his dirty fists on his hips and studied the flat tires on the passenger side of the Olds, strutted around and peered at the other flat tires. When he returned to stand facing Carver again, he said, "My, my, it 'pears somebody don't like you."

Carver said, "I've got an idea who."

"Well, they done a good job. For certain ruined them tires. Shame, too, as there was plenty of rubber left on 'em."

"Can you tow the car in and get some replacement tires on it soon as possible?"

"Sure, but soon as possible's sometime this afternoon."

"That'll be fine." Had to be.

Beth walked out of the room and stood behind Carver. Murray looked at her, then back at Carver. "Hey, you two're the ones I heard about did a number on the Brainard brothers at Whiffy's."

Beth said, not without pride, "That's us."

"Well, Christ, ain't no wonder you got your tires slashed. Fuck them Brainards, they always fuck back."

Beth said, "Get the tires fixed and we'll be outa here and they can fuck themselves."

Murray grinned at her with bold admiration. A couple of missing front teeth lent him a devilish look. "I'd advise it. Advise you to flag down the next Greyhound bus if one came through here. Sell me this old car cheap an' forget it, count yourselves lucky to get outa here without bein' worked on like them poor tires." He shook his head. "Michelins, too."

Beth tucked her fingertips in the back pockets of her Levi's and smiled at Murray. The way she was standing caused her elbows to brace backward and made her heavy breasts jut out aggressively. Carver wondered if she was working on poor Murray. She said, "Will the Brainless brothers object to you repairing the car so we can leave here?"

"Heh! Heh! The Brainless brothers, huh?" Clearly, Murray liked Beth. "They might object, but who gives a flyin' leap? Them two are the kinda worthless swamp turkeys don't work for a livin' an' make fun of folks that do. They don't like me turnin' an honest dollar, piss on 'em." He puffed out his chest again, like a proud pigeon, and strutted toward the truck to work the winch. "Only question's whether I got four tires this size."

Carver said, "Any size that fits the rims will do."

Murray started the electric winch and played out chain. Then he got down on all fours to fit the tow hooks to the car's frame. He said, "Wait a friggin' minute," and scampered to his feet.

Carver limped toward him. "What's the matter?"

Murray bent at the waist as if reaching to touch his toes. Amazingly limber. He rubbed at a white dusting on the gravel, then ran his thumb and forefinger together in a circling motion and frowned. After touching his finger to the tip of his tongue, like a chef testing a soufflé, he said, "Well, goddam!"

Carver watched as Murray loosened the Olds's gas cap. He stood staring into the fill pipe. Motioned Carver over with a wave of his grimy hand.

Murray said, "Looka this."

Carver looked and saw white granules around the edge of the fill pipe. He knew immediately what it was.

Murray screwed the gas cap back on. Both men listened as it made a grating sound. Murray said, "Some sonuvabitch poured sugar in your tank. Sugar don't dissolve in gasoline; you start this car up an' it'll get into the engine an' the metal parts'll grind themselves till they bind together. 'Scuse me for sayin' so, but it'd turn an old car like this the resta the way into junk. I mean, these vintage Olds's has got engines powerful as Arnold Schwartzen-whatever, but as you can see, rust is startin' to take over the body."

"So what do you have to do to get us on the road?" Carver asked.

"Aside from replacin' the tires, I gotta drain the gas tank. Take it off the car an' flush it out good. Drain the fuel line, too, just to make sure we got all the sugar outa the system. Then we let everything dry off good an' put it back together. Pump in some fresh gas, turn the key, an' hope we got it all an' the motor's the way God an' *De*-troit intended."

"How long's all that gonna take?" Carver asked.

"Realistically, you ain't goin' noplace till tomorrow mornin'. I ain't even sure I got tires'll fit. Might have to send outa town for some."

Carver stared out at the swamp, close and looming and green and thrumming with life and death. Something back in the ooze emitted a throaty, primitive cough. An alligator? "Okay," he said to Murray, "whatever it takes."

He gave Murray his Visa number, then watched as the Olds's back end was hoisted and Murray made sure the steering was locked.

When the tow truck dragging the raked, bouncing car had disappeared in a haze of dust, Beth said, "Guy's a kinda greasy Mr. Goodwrench."

"I hope so," Carver said. He did have the impression Murray knew cars. Loved them the way some men loved all women.

Dust settled in the sunlight, and Carver and Beth went back inside Carver's room.

They locked the doors and lay side by side on his bed, knowing they were stuck in Dark Glades, but glad to be out of the heat. They didn't make love, didn't even talk much, both of them listening to the labored, lulling hum of the air conditioner and thinking.

FINALLY, WHEN it was a few minutes past one, Carver got restless and climbed out of bed. Pacing around with his cane, he talked Beth into admitting she was hungry.

Then he borrowed Watt's battered Ford pickup, and they drove into town to get something to eat and check on whatever progress Murray was making with the Olds.

| 29 |

CARVER AND BETH returned to Whiffy's after Murray had run down a list of needed parts with a greasy, authoritative finger. He'd informed Carver he had only two tires in stock that would fit the Olds, then told him the car would be ready sometime tomorrow morning. Some kind of rare gasket and the tires were due in around sunup on a truck from Haines City.

Marlene the waitress kept their coffee cups filled. That was fine with Carver; he figured it wouldn't be a bad idea to stay up and alert most of the night, maybe in shifts. He and Beth let Whiffy entertain them with tales of dropped pop flies and outrageously called third strikes. To believe Whiffy was to be convinced that only a blind spot in his batting eye had prevented him from becoming another Hammering Henry Aaron, only better looking.

It was almost dark when Carver jockeyed Watts's old pickup truck back over the rutted dirt road to the motel. As he steered into the lot, he noticed three other cars parked in front of cabin doors. A long Lincoln with Canadian license plates, a red Toyota with clothes piled high on the backseat, and the blue Plymouth with the rental decal on its trunk. None of the guests were staying within two rooms' distance of Carver and Beth, Watts making sure that if anything did happen, victims would be kept to a minimum.

Carver parked the truck near the office, then sat and waited for the dieseling engine to *palump! palump!* to silence in the heat. The swamp was hard on things mechanical as well as people.

Beth opened the passenger-side door and hopped to the ground. Envying the way she could move, Carver struggled out of the truck with his cane.

He locked the truck, then limped into the office and saw Watts seated behind the desk, watching a ''Mayberry RFD'' rerun. Watts glanced over at Carver from his perch on a high stool. ''Goddam Barney's a scream, ain't he?''

Carver agreed, then dropped the truck keys on the desk. ''Thanks, Watts.''

''Car wasn't ready, I s'pose.'' Watts didn't avert his eyes from the TV. Barney had bought a used motorcycle and was showing it to a skeptical Sheriff Andy.

''It'll be ready tomorrow,'' Carver said. ''Anything happen around here?''

''Nope. No messages, no gunfire.''

Beth had gotten tired of standing in the doorway. She walked all the way into the office and stood near Carver, gazing over at the TV. She said, ''I always thought Barney was a prick.''

Watts looked at her as if she'd spat on a holy object. ''Hey, he's just a harmless little deputy.''

''Yeah? You get hassled by assholes like that and see how harmless they strike you.''

Watts stared at her and chewed the inside of his cheek, then gave her a nod as if maybe she had a point.

Carver watched as Barney sped away on the motorcycle, leaving the embarrassed sheriff sitting in the sidecar that had come unattached. Watts howled. The laugh track liked it even more. Carver grinned. Beth shook her head sadly.

Carver said, ''We'll be in our rooms the rest of the night.'' He limped toward the door.

Watts waved a hand in acknowledgment, engrossed in something Floyd, the Mayberry barber, was saying.

As they were walking across the gravel lot to their doors, Beth said, "What now, a holding action?"

Carver ran the backs of his knuckles gently down her cheek. "Sounds like a good idea."

She shoved his hand away. "Get serious, Carver."

He was, he thought. He said, "We'll lock ourselves in tight, put the Uzi and the Colt by the bed, and in the morning we'll drive Watts's truck in and pick up the Olds. Murray said he'd drive the truck back for us."

"You make it sound simple."

"Should work; the Brainard brothers *are* simple."

She laughed. "So's the atomic bomb, once you hear it explained. Still lethal, though."

Carver considered pointing out that she was the one who originally wouldn't leave Dark Glades. Then he decided he'd better not. They'd both underestimated the homicidal sincerity of the Brainards.

Insects were screaming. Carver waved away what felt like a moth fluttering against his face and paused, peering into the night. The dark swamp lay around them, like entangled terrain of the mind, the genesis of nightmares.

He was hot and coated with oily sweat. Suddenly he had a hard time breathing the thick, damp air and wanted to get out of it.

He quickly unlocked the door to his room. Opened it and limped inside. Flicked the light switch, then leaned on his cane while Beth came in. He closed the door and carefully locked it with the knob latch, the dead bolt, and the chain lock. The solid clicking and snicking of the locks made him feel more secure, even though he knew Junior Brainard could jolt the door off its hinges with one kick. The locks, the four walls, kept the swamp at bay, held off the nightmare.

Their packed suitcases were still on the floor, where they'd been left after Carver discovered the Olds's slashed tires. There was something unsettling about the abandoned luggage. All packed up and no place to go.

Beth said, "I need some stuff outa my bag. Toothpaste, nail polish."

Her body gave a slight jerk and she stared down at the Gucci suitcase.

Carver tightened his grip on his cane. "What's the matter?"

"A piece of a dress is caught in the zipper. I think my suitcase has been opened."

Carver and Beth both moved toward the suitcase. Beth was bending over it when the connecting door to her room opened.

Junior waddled in, cradling a high-powered rifle. B.J. followed. He was holding Beth's Uzi submachine gun aimed at Carver.

Junior grinned like a schoolkid about to pull wings off flies. "Betcha we know what you're lookin' for."

B.J.'s lean face was creased leather. He said, "We found it"—gave the Uzi a little bounce in his hands—"but we never found that handgun of yours, Carver. Be so kind as to get it out from under your shirt or wherever and lay it down there on the bed."

Carver didn't move. Beth had straightened up beside him. He could hear her tight, rapid breathing.

B.J. said, "I squeeze this trigger and your heart'll be hamburger. Nigger'll be next to go, only slower."

Junior said, "Lots slower."

Carver raised his untucked shirt. Holding the Colt delicately between thumb and forefinger, he drew it from his waistband and laid it on the bed. Junior swaggered over and picked it up. He examined it briefly but intensely, as if it were a new toy, then poked it down in his bib overalls. He was shirtless beneath the denim bib and straps of the dirty overalls; his stale body odor filled he room as if the fetid rot of the swamp had intruded.

B.J. said, "We figured it'd be a good idea to let ourselves in afore you locked us out. So we jimmied the bathroom window in the bitch's room and in we came. Been waitin' for you about an hour." He spat on the floor. Smiled. "You was about to lock the connecting door and barricade it, wasn't you?"

"You guessed it."

Junior said, "We wasn't gonna let you do that. One sign

of it and we'd'a come bustin' in here like the fuckin' SWAT team.''

Carver said, "Now that you're here, what?''

"First thing,'' B.J. said, "is you toss that cane on the bed next to the gun, then you move away and sit yourself down on the floor over there by the wall. Nigger'll sit next to you.''

Carver obeyed. He placed the cane on the bed, then jackknifed his body at the waist and used the mattress for support as he edged toward the wall.

"No, no,'' Junior said. "Go ahead an' crawl, fuckin' cripple. First night we seen you, we knew you was gonna crawl.''

"Best do it,'' B.J. said laconically. Carver heard the Uzi's action snick.

He dropped down and crawled the last few steps, dragging his stiff leg behind him, then sat down and leaned his back against the wall. Beth glared furiously at Junior, then sashayed over as if she were in control of things and lowered herself to sit next to Carver.

Junior plopped his bulk down in the room's one chair, making it groan in helpless protest. B.J. sat on the end of the bed. Both of them were staring at Carver and Beth in a way Carver didn't like. He knew they had ceased to be people to the Brainard brothers; they were business now. To be disposed of in a way the Brainards would enjoy, but still business. Mercy would play no part in it.

The night insects screamed louder. Bullfrogs croaked behind the motel. B.J. said, "We're gonna wait right here till it gets darker.''

"Then what?'' Beth asked. Carver heard her throat work as she swallowed. She laced her long fingers together and tightened them. She couldn't hide her fear.

Junior's imagination raced ahead. He grunted like a hog in sexual thrall.

B.J. grinned at Beth and traced a slow, tight circle in the air with the nasty barrel of the Uzi.

He said, "Yeah, then what?''

30

WHEN IT was midnight, B.J. and Junior led Carver and Beth outside at gunpoint. There were no lights in the motel other than the softly glowing road sign with the neon outline of the Spanish castle. Carver's cane had been returned to him. He was sure no one saw them as they crossed the gravel parking lot and walked along the dirt road through the swamp.

They turned onto a narrower, rutted side road. Walking was difficult in the dark. Carver's pace with the cane slowed them down, and he feigned more difficulty than he was having, trying to gain time to think. The swamp was black and ominous and screaming around them. Wing and fang and claw. Now and then Carver heard a splash and wondered what had made it. He was sweating from heat and fear. His shirt was plastered to his flesh, and insects flitted against him and occasionally bit or stung his bare arms. Beth was moving easily beside him. She had her fingers hooked in his belt almost casually, as if she might catch him if he started to fall. He could hear B.J. and Junior trudging heavily behind them. Now and then Junior would say, "Jus' keep on walkin'. Walk on . . . walk on." A kind of chant that was perversely soothing.

Suddenly B.J. said, "Hold it. Gotta look around here afore we go on."

Carver felt a gun barrel prod the small of his back, causing an ache in his spine.

He stood leaning on his cane, putting on a rapid-breathing act, as if he were exhausted from the walk over rough terrain. His daily bouts with the ocean had given him stamina. He could take this. This and more. He glanced up. Saw no stars. He and Beth looked at each other with blank faces that denied panic. They were wrapped in thick foliage in the deep swamp.

"Over there," B.J. said. He shoved Carver toward a blacker shadow just off the road. High and boxy. It was the knobby-tired Blazer.

Carver and Beth sat on the rubber-matted floor in back while Junior kept the Uzi trained on them. B.J. drove.

The inside of the Blazer smelled like oil and rotted fish. Tools or fishing equipment rattled around in a pad-locked, battered steel box bolted to the floor behind the seats. Blackness pressed against the windows. There was no way to gauge direction, but the rumbling, bucking truck made several sharp turns. A front window was open, but it admitted only the saturated warmth of the swamp, along with mosquitoes, and occasional large beetlelike bugs that ricocheted crazily around the inside of the truck and dropped, buzzing and dying, on the floor.

After about fifteen minutes, B.J. braked the Blazer to a jarring halt. The abrupt stop caused Beth's head to bounce off the side window. She gave no indication she'd felt it.

Junior grinned in the shadows behind the black eye of the Uzi's bore. Said, "Home."

B.J. got out first, then stood behind the Blazer while Carver and Beth crawled out the back. Beth helped Carver until he was standing with his weight bearing down on the cane. For a moment her mouth was near his ear and he thought she might whisper something, but she was silent.

They were in a clearing lit faintly by moonlight and surrounded by saw grass and towering cypress trees. There was a rambling, flat-roofed shack with a falling-down porch. A very old, block-long Cadillac was parked in front of it. Off to the left was a post-and-wire fence. The posts jutted crookedly from the ground like spindly broken fingers, but the wire was taut and appeared barbed. A cluster of small animals stood inside the fence. Goats, Carver thought, though he could only make out vague shapes in the moon shadows.

He knew they were a long way from civilization here. A long way from help. Beth seemed to sense it, too. She shivered beside him in the hot swamp air.

Junior was still holding the Uzi. Still grinning. His porcine little eyes were glittering diamonds in the moonlight. "Know what we use them goats for?" he asked.

Carver said, "Not keeping the grass short, I bet."

"There's a bet you'd win," B.J. said. He was waving the rifle barrel slowly to sweep the space between Carver and Beth. He could nudge the barrel either way and put a bullet through one or the other in an instant. Carver thought he might be able to inch near enough to lash out with the cane, maybe knock the rifle aside or out of B.J.'s grip, but then brother Junior would open up with the Uzi. The Brainards had it figured. This was their game.

Junior said, "We take them goats one at a time an' stake 'em out at night at a place near here. 'Gators hear 'em when they bleat, come up outa the swamp to feed on 'em. When a big enough 'gator's busy with his meal, B.J. an' me open up with rifles an' get us enough alligator hide to make somebody a suit." He rolled his tongue around the inside of his cheek, looking for a moment as if he were chewing a wad of tobacco, then spat. "Killin' 'em might be illegal, but they's good money in 'gators," he finished, as if defending his poaching.

"Not to mention fun," B.J. said.

Junior said, "Gonna be the most fun tonight."

Carver felt his good leg turn to rubber. He leaned hard on the cane. Beth moved closer to him, so her hip and thigh were touching his. She'd realized the direction of the Brainards' revenge. He could feel the vibration of her trembling.

She said, "You bastards!"

Junior giggled, sounding like a hog that had been tickled.

B.J. said, "Save your insults for the 'gators, nigger."

He motioned with the rifle barrel. "Now, the two of you walk straight ahead, into the swamp. I'll tell you when to stop."

Beth moved slowly while Carver limped beside her, along what seemed to be a narrow path. Leaves brushed his arms and face. Something that felt like a web settled on his neck and he brushed it off. His fingers touched a large insect for an instant; brittle wings whirred and he heard it buzz and drop to the ground behind him. A beetle like the ones that had flitted into the Blazer? "Walk on . . . walk on," Junior muttered. Carver set the tip of his cane carefully. The ground was getting softer, soggy. Off on either side of the path, he could hear things moving in water. The swamp lapped at the saw grass and the exposed roots of the giant cypress trees that twisted grotesquely in the darkness. One of the brothers shoved Carver forward when he paused to find a dry spot for the tip of his cane. Carver almost fell. He caught himself by levering the cane into the damp ground. It made a sucking sound when he withdrew it from the mud. Beth said again, "Bastards!"

B.J. produced a flashlight from where it was stuck in his belt beneath his shirt. He switched it on, then swept the beam from side to side like a lance that met hard shadow and was turned away. Blackness and thick foliage curved around them. Once, Carver was sure the yellow beam swept past a pair of luminous eyes. Beth hadn't seen them; she was busy helping Carver maintain his footing on the softening earth.

"They's quicksand around here," Junior said, and giggled again. He was up for something tonight, was Junior.

They walked on toward the center of the darkness.

After what seemed like half an hour they were in another clearing. This one was smaller. A tall, angled tree grew near the middle of it. The grass was flattened around the tree. The flashlight beam lingered on a thick rope wound around the trunk.

B.J. said, "This here's the place, folks."

Junior moved around to stand in front and off to the side of Carver. He aimed the Uzi at him at gut level and said, "You move, asshole, I'm gonna cut you in half. Leave you for 'gator food."

B.J. planted a hand in the center of Beth's back and shoved her toward the tree. Pushed her again as she stumbled and tried to catch her balance. On her knees, she glared up at him in the moonlight, then spat at him. He raked the rifle barrel across her head. A trickle of blood, black in the dim light, snaked down her cheek. He dug the long barrel into her back, forcing her to lie flat on her stomach in the beaten down grass. Carver noticed a bare white bone on the ground near her left shoulder. Helpless rage flared in him as he looked into Junior's fat grinning face.

Spreading his feet wide, B.J. stretched out an arm and nimbly unwound about five feet of the rope that encircled the tree. Then he knelt with his knee in the small of Beth's back and skillfully used the rope to bind her wrists behind her. It was like an event at a rodeo; took no more than half a minute.

B.J. stood up, letting the rifle point at the ground as he stared down at Beth. He smiled dreamily in the moonlight and said, "She ain't goin' nowhere. Not ever again."

Beth sat up and twisted her body awkwardly. Struggled against the rope for a moment and seemed to realize she couldn't escape. There was no way to free her arms. Her body bent, she waddled in a circle around the tree to unwind the rope, but it was knotted so only a few more feet played out and she couldn't stand upright.

B.J. stepped close to her and slapped her hard on the cheek. Then he gripped the top of her blouse and ripped it halfway off. The parting material made a sound like a hoarse whistle.

Carver took a step toward them. Junior raised the Uzi, looking as if he wanted to use it. "Stay right fuckin' there, tough man. You wanna watch, don't you?"

Carver took a deep breath. It was all he could do not to strike out with the cane and hurl himself at Junior, try for the Uzi so he could open up on B.J. But Junior kept just the right distance between them. The drug trade, or maybe the military, had taught him how to restrain someone with a gun.

Unable to move, Carver couldn't look away from what was going on beneath the branches of the tilted tree.

Beth kicked furiously at B.J. and he laughed. He caught a leg and hoisted it suddenly so she fell on her back, on her bound wrists. He unzipped her Levi's and worked them down around her ankles so she couldn't kick. Then he tore off her bikini panties, looked thoughtfully at them, and stuffed them in his pocket. He pulled off the rest of her blouse except for a few tatters, and removed her bra with an odd gentleness. Then he yanked her Levi's the rest of the way off, sending her muddy shoes flying, and stood back in triumph as if to admire his work.

Junior rubbed his crotch with his free hand. Under his breath he said, "Gonna be fun for sure."

B.J., breathing hard from his efforts, stared at Beth and said, "Ain't such a rough bitch now, are you, nigger?"

Beth said, "Fuck you, you backwater bumpkin!"

B.J. shook his head. "Jesus, ain't you somethin'? Don't you fuckin' know what's gonna happen to you?"

Beth was quiet. She sat with her knees drawn up to partly cover her breasts. The moonlight highlighted her long, lush body and made her look as vulnerable as she was. Her painted toes curled down into the mud. She was gazing at Carver, something tight inside her controlling the terror that was in her eyes.

Junior moved around in front of Carver and waved the Uzi. "Walk on over there," he said, as B.J. swaggered across the clearing to stand behind him.

Carver hobbled along the narrow path until Junior said, "Far enough. Now ease on over to your right, 'neath that tree. In deep amongst them big roots."

Water seeped into his shoes as Carver obeyed. He could hear the soggy ground squishing beneath his soles. His cane found little support and was almost useless.

Then he was leaning in the gnarled wood jumble of cypress roots, trapped as if he were in a grotesquely distorted cage.

Junior wedged in close behind him. Carver could feel his warm, anxious breathing, smell his sour breath. Junior had eaten onions lately, drunk beer. B.J. had the Uzi now.

He settled down in a siting position on a horizontal stretch
of exposed root.

Carver could barely move; Junior was pressing him from
behind, and an elbow of hard wood was digging into his
stomach.

B.J. and Junior had spent time here before and knew
the place as a vantage point. From the tangle of thick
cypress root they could see through the darkness to where
Beth sat curled beneath the tree, her shoulders hunched
and her hands bound behind her. She was motionless, her
head bowed, as if what was happening had finally caught
up with her and mercifully sent her into shock.

Carver heard what sounded like Junior licking his lips.
Felt a revulsion and hatred he hadn't thought possible.

B.J., as wily as Junior, kept a safe distance with the
Uzi. Stark shadow turned his bony face into a death's head.
Still breathing hard from struggling with Beth, he pressed
a thumb to the side of his nose, blew noisily, and flicked
snot away. He wiped his hands on his pants and glanced
in Beth's direction. Back at Carver.

He said, "Now we settle down an' wait. Pretty soon,
somethin'll come."

31

WHAT CAME into the clearing was something long and wet and gleaming dully in the moonlight. First a blunt snout, then a pair of bulbous eyes, then the rest of the alligator. It made no sound as it slithered from the tall saw grass and lay still, peering at Beth, who hadn't yet noticed it.

"Bitch didn't even scream nor make any noise," Junior whispered.

B.J. said, "She surely will scream. 'Gator musta been watchin' us all along from the dark."

"It's a big'n," Junior said, admiring the alligator. "Least nine, ten foot long."

There was a faint splashing sound, and another, much smaller alligator eased into the clearing. The moon sent shimmers off its rough, wet flank. It bared its rows of pointed teeth, a ghastly ivory grin in the faint light.

Beth must have heard the splashing. She raised her head and looked at the small alligator, which was no more than three feet long. Her body grew rigid and, legs pumping, she scooted back against the tree. She wriggled in a final attempt to free her hands, then sat staring at the small alligator. It stared back at her.

Carver whispered, "Christ, don't let this happen!"

Junior said, "What's this? You beggin', tough man?"

"Call it that if you want," Carver said. "Don't let her die this way. Please!"

"Gonna be some sight to see," Junior said.

B.J. said, "Shut the fuck up, both of you." A hoarse command.

The large alligator seemed to notice the smaller one. It suddenly raised itself on surprisingly long, bent legs and hissed loudly. Beth's head jerked around. She saw the huge creature and her eyes widened. Her mouth gaped. She tried to scream; Carver could see her throat working. But she made no sound. The huge 'gator hissed again and switched its tail.

Beth thrashed against her bonds.

Encouraged by her desperate movements, the big alligator started to drag itself toward her in a terrible lizard waddle. It seemed to be moving slowly, but it was covering ground fast.

Junior pressed his thick body against Carver and prodded the base of Carver's skull with the rifle barrel. "No noise now, tough man, lest I—"

His body gave a slight jerk. He said, "What the shit? . . ." and began convulsing against Carver. The rifle barrel slid off to the side like an errant compass needle.

Carver was aware there'd been a shot. He turned and looked into Junior's glazing eyes, feeling something warm and wet against his back. He knew it was blood; he could smell the coppery stench of it.

B.J. said, "What the hell's goin' on?" He moved out from the tangle of cypress roots. Carver saw that the big alligator had been frozen by the sound of the shot.

B.J. caught sight of Junior, who'd slumped to an awkward lean. He stared at him in disbelief, then at Carver. "You motherfucker!" he screamed, and bared his teeth like the alligator. Apparently he thought Carver had somehow wrested the rifle from Junior and shot him. He leveled the Uzi at Carver.

Carver yelled, " 'Gator! 'Gator!"

B.J. only half believed him, but had to chance a backward look.

Another shot sounded from the blackness of the swamp.

B.J. spun around, then staggered out into the clearing.

There was a third shot, like a dull handclap muffled by the thick night. Carver saw B.J.'s head jerk to the side and back, as if he were trying to flip his hair out of his eyes. The Uzi discharged half a dozen chattering rounds into the ground.

Carver had grabbed the rifle and eased himself out from in front of Junior's inert bulk. Junior, propped upright in the tangle of thick roots, seemed to be watching him, drooling in the shadowed, yellow light.

Carver trained the rifle on B.J., but the lanky swamp man had survived his brother by only a few seconds. He lay on his back with his arms flung wide and his legs splayed out, as if he'd dropped lifeless from high up.

The staccato bark of the Uzi must have scared the alligators back into the swamp. The clearing was empty except for Beth, who was staring numbly at Carver, not comprehending. The whites of her eyes showed all the way around her dark pupils. There was a horror in those eyes that tore at his heart.

He rushed to her and dug his fingernails into the damp rope that was looped and knotted tightly around her wrists. He managed to loosen a knot. Another.

"Listen!" he was saying to her. "Listen. We gotta get outa here! Can you understand me?"

He thought she nodded, but he couldn't be sure. He kept working on the knots with painful, stiffening fingers.

Didn't hear anyone approach.

"I'll take over, Carver," someone said.

He knew the voice.

Roberto Gomez.

Carver gripped his cane and turned, staring up at Gomez and Hirsh. Gomez was wearing khaki pants, a black or green pullover shirt, and rubber boots that laced tight around his tucked-in pants legs. Hirsh had on his dark, vested suit, and what looked like a pair of hip boots. The golden arc of his watch chain gleamed across his stomach paunch. Gomez was holding an Uzi like the one on the ground beside B.J.'s body. Hirsh was gripping a long dark revolver.

Hirsh said, "Toss the rifle out into the clearing and move away, Carver."

Carver hadn't realized the rifle he'd taken from Junior's dead hands was lying next to his extended bad leg. He picked it up by the stock and slung it over near B.J.'s corpse. Then he stood up slowly and limped across the soggy ground toward Gomez and Hirsh.

Hirsh said, "Far enough."

Carver stopped and stood still, centering his weight on the cane.

Gomez walked over and stood near Beth, who'd loosened the rope enough to slip her hands free. She sat rubbing her wrists, not looking up at Gomez.

He bent down and grabbed a handful of her hair, then yanked her head back so she had to look at him. After muttering something to her in Spanish, he spat in her face.

She bowed her head again and sat quietly, trembling.

Gomez bent down and picked up the loose end of the rope. He looked over at Hirsh and said, "This alligator idea couldn't be improved upon, eh?"

Hirsh said, "Doubt it. But what about the construction site?"

Gomez said to Carver, "He means a place where the highway department's gonna pour concrete tomorrow for a new section of road. Gonna be your grave, Carver, yours and Beth's. You two are gonna have a long, flat tombstone with a yellow line on it."

Hirsh said, "I don't think he cares for that idea, Mr. Gomez."

"Does it fucking matter?"

Hirsh looked over at Carver with his sad eyes. "Nope, don't matter a gnat's ass."

"We can do them here," Gomez said, "then stuff 'em in the trunk and drive 'em to the construction site. We got plastic in the trunk, don't we?"

"Always," Hirsh said.

"Then the 'gator gets a snack and we'll bury the leftovers." Gomez smiled at Carver. "What about it, my man? You think of a better way for a bitch like this to leave life?"

"If you can't think of one," Carver said, "why'd you stop it from happening? Why didn't you sit back and watch?"

Gomez narrowed his eyes at Carver and looked confused. He glanced at B.J., then turned to face Carver. "Hold on. *You* didn't shoot these swamp turkeys?"

Hirsh said, "Jesus!"

The big 'gator was back, at the edge of the clearing, standing amazingly tall on its long legs so it could see above the saw grass, baring its sharp teeth. It hissed. It didn't like to have its meal interrupted.

Hirsh couldn't help staring at the alligator. His mouth was hanging open as if he were imitating it.

Carver brought his cane down hard across Hirsh's wrist. The revolver dropped to the ground. Hirsh instinctively grabbed at the probably broken wrist and Carver crossed the cane over his neck. Heard and felt cartilage give.

Hirsh was down on his back, clutching his crushed larynx and thrashing his legs, gasping and choking and dying.

Beth screamed, "Carver!"

Carver saw Gomez swinging the barrel of the Uzi in his direction. He dived for Hirsh's revolver but couldn't find it. Hirsh must have fallen on it. Gomez was advancing on him now, the Uzi leveled, his eyes darting back and forth between the gagging and thrashing Hirsh, and Carver.

The huge 'gator hissed again. Gomez whipped his head around in the direction of the sound.

Carver had his chance. He flung his cane at Gomez and prepared to rush at him. The cane whispered as it cut the air.

Gomez must have sensed something. Or maybe heard the cane pinwheeling toward him.

He ducked.

The cane merely brushed his shoulder and dropped behind him.

He smiled at Carver. "Time for you to join the fucking swamp turkeys, my man."

Both of them heard the shot and paused. Glanced around.

Then Gomez realized he'd been hit. He grabbed at his chest. Tried to raise the Uzi but dropped it. He said, "Goddammit!" and sat down hard, then fell back and lay still.

Beth was standing up, holding on to the tree with both hands for balance. Staring beyond Carver.

Carver turned to see what she was looking at.

There was a rhythmic splashing sound.

Someone walking.

McGregor emerged from the swamp, cradling a hunting rifle and grinning.

The big alligator saw him and slithered on its lizard legs back into the blackness of nightmares. Surrendering the moonlit clearing to a more ferocious predator.

32

MCGREGOR COVERED ground in long, loose strides to within ten feet of Roberto Gomez. He carefully aimed the rifle. This time the shot was deafening. Gomez's body jerked as the bullet slammed into it. Things stirred in the dark swamp, alarmed by the shot, then were quiet. Gomez's outflung right arm twitched, but it had to be nerve reaction in an organism shutting itself down. He'd probably been dead when McGregor shot him the second time.

Carver looked at Beth, who was staring at McGregor almost the way she'd looked at the big alligator. McGregor glanced over at her. He was still grinning.

Carver said, "Meet McGregor."

She nodded stupidly, almost as if it were a social introduction to someone who awed and frightened her. McGregor affected some people that way. So did spiders.

His grin became a leer as his eyes traveled up and down Beth's nude form. He said, "So that's what it was all about, huh? Root of all evil, after money."

Carver lurched to where his cane lay, picked it up, and hobbled over to where Beth was leaning against the tree. He put his arm around her. Hugged her to him. Her body was rigid, unyielding. Then her breath trailed out of her and she sagged against him.

But only for a few seconds. Then her body shifted and

she was standing tall on her own. She was unashamed of her nakedness, seemingly unaware of it, a dark Eve in a darker Eden. She glared at McGregor as if he were the serpent.

He said, "You oughta thank me for saving your life, dumb cunt."

Carver said, "He shot the Brainard brothers. Roberto and Hirsh assumed *I* had. I assumed *they'd* done it."

"Me all along," McGregor said proudly. He pointed with the rifle at Hirsh's now motionless form. "That asshole dead?"

"He's dead," Carver said. He remembered the sound of crushed cartilage and Hirsh's gasping for air that couldn't reach his lungs. He didn't want to look at Hirsh's face.

McGregor glanced again at Hirsh, then at Carver. "You know some tricks, for a gimpy ex-cop with a lotta delusions."

Carver's mind kept chewing on something. "How'd you come to be here?" he asked. "How'd you find us?"

McGregor said, "How'd I *find* you? Shit! I knew where you were the day you left. Followed you to the Beame house and had the phone tapped. First time Elizabeth here called Melanie about her son, I was listening. Traced the call to this godforsaken place. I been staying at your motel, fuckhead. Watching the two of you."

Carver realized what McGregor had done. What it meant. Anger and bile rose bitterly in his throat. "Jesus! You've been waiting here in Dark Glades for Gomez to show."

"That's right," McGregor said, obviously pleased with himself. "You sure as fuck do have detecting skills. But then you know what they say about how even a blind pig'll find an acorn now and then. When you two ran and left the kid behind, you gave me a way to get *Gomez* to come to *me*, assface. All I had to do was drop a word and then stay close to you and the bitch here."

"Bait," Carver said. "You found out where we were, then you made sure Gomez found out, too. Then you came here and waited for him to show up and try to kill us."

"Bait?" McGregor said. "Yeah, I guess that's right. But don't forget, those two swamp creeps woulda done the both of you in if I hadn't come along. Not to mention your Gomez-and-Hirsh dilemma. Hell, I saved your asses twice over, and you're griping at me 'cause I used you for minnows that'd attract the big fish. Some gratitude." He leered again at Beth. The pink tip of his tongue peeked lewdly out from the wide gap between his front teeth.

"That's not exactly proper police procedure, is it?" Carver said. "Police aren't supposed to use citizens as bait, then mow down the bad guys from ambush without giving them a chance to surrender. You could lose your badge for that."

"Nobody'll know about two of the bad guys," McGregor said, still sneaking peeks at Beth. "That'll make my version and the odds seem plausible enough."

Carver peeled off his shirt and gave it to Beth. She slipped it on. It covered her nudity well enough, came halfway to her knees. She gripped the bottom of the shirt and stretched it to conceal even more of her. McGregor looked disappointed.

He said, "I was gonna bury these two bad-ass brothers in the swamp, but maybe that's not such a good idea. If anybody does look for them, the search'll be concentrated in this area. I think we'll take a cue from Gomez and drive them to the highway construction site. I know just where it is. Passed it on the way here."

"What about Gomez and Hirsh?" Carver asked, wondering how McGregor was going to twist what had happened to his advantage. Twist it so it might propel him all the way to the office of mayor of Del Moray, and maybe beyond. Public service, ethics, or compassion would play no part in it. Politics and McGregor were compatible because he thought big and acted small.

"We leave Gomez and Hirsh where they are," McGregor said. "The three of us drive the dead brothers to the construction site and bury them. Throw some dirt over them where concrete'll be poured tomorrow. We can use that camouflaged truck of theirs to transport them. Then we drive back here and pick up my car. Park the truck by the cabin. Whole thing shouldn't take more'n a couple hours. When we're done, I drive you back to the motel and phone the local law and the DEA. Report that I followed Gomez and Hirsh all the way here from Del Moray and into the swamp because I had a tip about a drug pickup. They realized I was there and we fought. Gomez tried to blast me, but I shot more accurately."

"Not to mention first," Carver said, "and from cover of darkness."

McGregor shrugged. "It'll be assumed the swamp brothers were involved in the drug deal and disappeared. What I heard about them, nobody'll much give a fuck what happened to them."

"What if the alligators come back and drag away Gomez and Hirsh? Make a meal of them?"

"There's always leftovers," McGregor said. "Have faith in Forensics."

"And you'll be a hero," Carver said. He had to admire McGregor's audacity, but there was an obstacle. Two obstacles. "What makes you think your secret'll be safe with us?"

McGregor's lascivious grin crawled back onto his face. "Remember, Carver, you haven't behaved very ethically in this. You got your livelihood to protect. As for the cunt, here, I'll see to it she can testify in a secret, closed hearing. The law's gonna make her spill her guts anyway, but this way there'll be no publicity, and Gomez's drug buddies won't know about it and track her down and kill her."

"You really think you can swing that kinda deal for her?"

"*Know* I can. She's got knowledge to trade, and I'll be the fucking man of the hour." The moon glowed in his pale, sly eyes. "Only smart thing for her to do."

"Maybe," Carver said. A mosquito lit on the back of his hand. He flicked it away, but not before it drew blood.

"Then there's the matter of the cocaine," McGregor said.

"Cocaine?"

"The cocaine I brought along so if you two don't co-operate I can say I got it outa your motel room. Gomez's wife corrupted you, is the way the story'll go. Promised you some of the big drug money if you'd help her. The two of you, here near the scene of a major drug deal, a possession charge won't be easy for you to fight.''

Carver looked at Beth, who was staring at McGregor with loathing and disbelief.

"He's right," Carver told her. "And he'd do what he's threatening. I know him. He would.''

Beth said, "He's worse than the people Roberto knows. Knew.''

McGregor's grin widened as if he'd been complimented. He said, "Okay, let's get busy. We'll get the plastic sheets Gomez mentioned outa the trunk of the limo. It's parked up near the Brainards' shack. We'll roll the brothers in plastic, then we'll toss some dirt over them at the construction site. By tomorrow afternoon, they'll be safe under two feet of concrete highway, where they always wanted to be—in the fast lane.''

McGregor reached into Hirsh's hip pocket and pulled out the key to the limo. Beth retrieved her shoes, and she and Carver followed McGregor to the shack.

The limo hadn't been able to make it all the way over the rutted road. It was parked about a hundred yards from the shack. They got the folded plastic sheets from its cavernous trunk, even a couple of shiny new shovels; Gomez and Hirsh had come prepared for everything but their own deaths.

Already perspiring heavily in the hot night, they walked back to the clearing and stood over B.J. Brainard's body. Carver said, "He'll be no trouble, but Junior won't be easy to drag back to the Blazer.''

"The three of us can manage," McGregor said. "It'll get done. Before morning these two'll be underground, I'll be back here with a shitpot full of DEA and local law, and you two'll be back in your room at the motel. I can goddam well make this work. You don't believe me, assface, just watch and see.''

Carver said, "Somehow I believe you.''

"Then unfold those plastic drop cloths or whatever the fuck they are. Pick up the guns and wrap them in with the bodies.'' He turned to Beth. ''You carry my rifle. Leave Gomez's and Hirsh's weapons where they are. Got it?''

Beth said she did. She stared down at her dead husband. Her features were impassive. It was impossible to guess what she was thinking. What she was reliving.

McGregor said, ''Remember he was gonna feed you to the alligators.''

Beth surprised Carver. She nudged Gomez's corpse with the toe of her shoe and said, ''I remember. And further back than tonight. Good riddance, Roberto.''

McGregor looked at her with a flicker of approval.

Carver and McGregor got the bodies wrapped. Carver retrieved his Colt from where it was stuck in Junior's belt and shoved it down his waistband at the small of his back. Then he picked up the Uzi the Brainards had confiscated from Beth, and a rifle, and wound them in plastic along with B.J.'s body.

B.J. wasn't much of a problem. McGregor slung his plastic-clad corpse across his shoulders and carried him fireman-fashion to the truck while Carver and Beth trudged along behind.

McGregor found an old wheelbarrow in a toolshed near the shack, and they used it to transport Junior. Even then, they spent most of their time carrying him over soft mud, and Beth had to help several times when the wheelbarrow's narrow wheel sank into the ooze.

They loaded the bodies in the cargo area of the Blazer. Carver sat in back with them and watched while McGregor opened the trunk of the blue Plymouth that had been parked at the motel. Beth dropped the rifle into the dark trunk, and McGregor hurriedly slammed down the lid and made sure the trunk was locked.

McGregor drove the heavily laden four-wheel-drive Blazer out of the swamp and to the interstate highway. He maneuvered the ruts and bumps as if he'd spent his entire life in Dark Glades. Like so many egomaniacs, he could rise to necessity and find dormant talents.

In less than an hour they'd reached the deserted construction site, and shortly thereafter the Brainards were buried like plastic-shrouded mummies in shallow graves.

Clouds had closed in. The night was almost totally black, and only infrequent sets of speeding headlights, like tracer bullets on the distant detour, broke the darkness. The grisly job was completed in privacy.

When the last shovelful of loose earth had been tossed, McGregor stood back and placed a hand over his heart, his head bowed. For a moment Carver actually thought he was going to say a few words over the graves. What he said was, "Better thee than me, assholes." Then he laughed. "Ready? Let's get the fuck outa here."

Carver was ready.

CARVER AND BETH stayed in Carver's room at the Casa Grande that night. They heard distant sirens. McGregor, having a high time with Chief Morgan and the DEA. With the news media. A hero being born.

Beth snuggled close to Carver. They'd showered together, and she smelled like perfumed soap and shampoo. She said, "You think McGregor can really make it work?"

Carver said, "Trust him."

And fell asleep.

AT WHIFFY'S the next morning, the talk was of nothing other than what had happened in the swamp near the Brainards' shack. How a big-time drug dealer and his partner had been killed during some kind of narcotics transaction, but the Brainards had escaped. Behind the long counter, Whiffy looked briefly at Carver and Beth and offered the opinion that Dark Glades had seen the last of the Brainards. Several customers agreed, and opined that that was just fine.

Carver and Beth ate their bacon and eggs silently, enjoying the cool breeze from the ticking ceiling fan.

Over fresh coffee, Beth stared across the table at Carver and said, "Guess I better tell you."

He saw it in her eyes, though he didn't understand it. Felt something cold close in on him. A premonition. "Tell me what?"

She inhaled and held her breath for several seconds, as

if not wanting to turn the words loose. Then she said, "Adam's not my son. He's Melanie's."

Carver couldn't believe it. He set down his cup too hard, almost breaking it against the saucer as he sloshed hot coffee onto his thumb. He sat back and stared at her.

Beth said, "I sorta borrowed Adam. Got Melanie to cooperate."

"And your real son?"

"He died in childbirth. Not from drug addiction complications, but because he was a breech birth and the umbilical cord got wrapped around his neck. It was asphyxiation."

"Roberto knew this?"

"No. I planted the heroin addiction story, just like I said. I didn't know it'd turn him into an animal, out for revenge. Didn't realize how ferociously he'd hunt me and try to kill me."

"He was an animal to begin with, and he thought you killed his son."

Beth bowed her head and began to sob quietly. "Christ, I don't know, maybe I *did*. Maybe it happened because of the life I led. Because I let myself get pregnant by somebody like Roberto in the first place. He didn't love me; he only married me for legal reasons—so I could refuse to testify against him if push came to shove in court. I was heartbroken when our baby died, but I saw it as an opportunity to get away. You don't walk out on a man like Roberto; a marriage is over when *he* says so. If I got by with the heroin story, I figured he wouldn't want me after the baby dying with an addiction, and that he'd think I'd be dead in a short while anyway, so he wouldn't come looking for me. I was wrong."

Carver said, "Jesus, you were wrong! About everything." He tried to take a sip of coffee but found his hand was trembling too much. He placed the cup back in its saucer, gently this time, listening to the brief music of china on china as his hand shook. "You got me going, though. One lie after another."

"Would you have helped me otherwise?" she asked calmly and sadly.

"No," he admitted. The truth cut him like a blade. "If the baby's not yours, why did you call Melanie from the motel?"

"I needed to keep you convinced, and I wanted to make sure Roberto hadn't traced our moves and harmed Melanie for helping me."

"You are something," Carver said. "An actress good enough for the movies."

Beth sat up straighter. She rubbed her eyes with the heels of her hands, as if she were infinitely weary, then gave Carver the look of a woman twenty years older. "I did what I had to in order to survive. Can't you understand that?"

He said, "I do understand."

"Then can you forgive me?"

Carver said, "No. I'm sorry, but I can't."

Another thing he couldn't do was look at her. He put down a ten-dollar bill to cover breakfast and a tip and stood up, then he limped out of there. She let him leave without calling to him.

Well, she was finished using him.

On the drive back to Del Moray he listened to the news on the Olds's radio. McGregor was selling his story to the DEA and the media. Carver hadn't doubted he would, but still he was impressed. The force of McGregor's evil and ego was such that it engulfed and persuaded.

Carver had heard enough. He switched off the radio and settled back in the sun-warmed vinyl seat. The car's canvas top was down. He draped a wrist over the top of the steering wheel and let the wind swirl around him.

As he drove past the highway construction site, he saw a procession of cement trucks with their mixers slowly revolving, lined along the dirt shoulder and inching forward as their stacks belched dark diesel fumes. One by one pouring the Brainard brothers' gravestone.

| 33 |

IT HAD BEEN three months since Carver said good-bye to
Edwina at the airport in Orlando. He'd stood and watched
the swept-wing airliner rise in two-hundred-mile-per-hour
slow motion from the runway, its engines trailing a haze
of jet exhaust, and knew he'd never see her again. They'd
been lovers, but they'd said good-bye as if they were
strangers.

Beth Gomez had given the DEA secret depositions, and
there'd been an unprecedented series of drug busts in Florida, as well as in Georgia and Louisiana. The Brainard
brothers continued their forever sleep beneath a highway
that, in Florida's endless summer, would last beyond their
natural span of years. Far into the next century, their bones
might be discovered when the highway finally was repaved
or repaired. By then, who and what they were would no
longer matter, and the lives of everyone involved would
have played out and been pushed into minor history by
time.

Carver continued to work out of his office on Magellan
Avenue, and he'd taken several cases. One was divorce
work, two others were industrial theft. None of them was
a challenge. He found himself doing the kind of drone
work that reminded him of when he was with the Orlando
police. Mostly he stayed around his beach cottage, watch-

ing the sea roll in and roll out, and feeling his life ebb and wear with the ponderous and relentless rush of the ocean. He was drinking too often, not shaving often enough.

Now and then Desoto would come to see him and they'd sit and sip beer and watch the sea, and Desoto would try to goad him from his lethargy. Desoto knew what was bothering Carver even more than the parting with Edwina.

Maybe Desoto had something to do with what happened at dusk on a hot, damp day when Carver was lying in bed and staring at the ceiling. He heard the screen door squeak open and closed, but he didn't bother turning his head to see who'd entered. Not that many people came to visit. Probably if he looked he'd see Johnny the beach prowler, who liked to drop by and talk with Carver and show him his day's haul of interesting shells and lost jewelry and coins. Or maybe he'd see Desoto.

Beth's voice said, "You look like something the cat'd drag *out*, Carver."

He rolled his head and focused his eyes on her. She was wearing a pale yellow dress and white high heels, had her hair pulled back. Looked fantastic. He felt something stir in him, sending tentacles through his mind to touch places he'd wanted to forget existed.

He said, "Didn't expect visitors," and resented the way his voice almost broke. The way he couldn't look away from her.

She took a few elegant strides farther inside the cabin, like a queen surrounded by squalor. Standing in the soft light, she stared down at him the way people stare at furniture they think might be worth refinishing. He could smell her perfume—familiar, disturbing, pushing buttons in his memory.

She said, "McGregor's not going to run for mayor."

"That doesn't surprise me," Carver told her.

"Why not?"

"That night in the swamp, the rifle I handed you to put in the trunk of his car wasn't McGregor's, it was the Brainards'. McGregor's rifle is wrapped in plastic and buried along with B.J. Brainard under the highway."

Beth propped her hands on her hips and smiled down at him, figuring it out fast. "And the bullets in the Brainard brothers will match the rifle, which is registered to McGregor and is the gun that killed Roberto."

"That's it," Carver said. "McGregor knows if he runs for mayor, I can see that the brothers' bodies are discovered."

"Wouldn't that put you in jeopardy too? I mean, you'd be an accessory after the fact."

"Yeah, but McGregor's not sure I wouldn't tip the law anyway."

"Would you?"

Carver didn't answer. Instead he said, "Were the last few months rough for you?"

"Sometimes. Better'n the alternative. Who can ask for more than that?"

He rolled his head again on the perspiration-damp pillow and gazed up at the too-familiar network of cracks in the ceiling. A wasp was crawling around up there; he remembered it buzzing and darting at the window this afternoon, seeking light and a way out.

Beth sighed and said, "I heard about the way you been pissing away your life out here. If you don't wanna jump up outa that bed right now, it's okay with me. But I gotta know."

"Oh? Know what?"

"What I came here to find out. Whether you want me to go or stay."

Without looking at her, Carver said, "Stay, please."

She got undressed and climbed into the bed with him. The springs squealed wildly. She draped a long, dark leg over both of his, flung an arm across him. Then she rested her head on his chest and cried softly. They both could feel what was happening, and it made them sad and afraid and joyful all at the same time.

Lakes turning.

Seasons changing.

JAMES ELLROY

"Echoes the Best of Wambaugh"
New York Sunday News

BROWN'S REQUIEM   **78741-5/$3.95 US $4.95 Can**
Join ex-cop and sometimes P.I. Fritz Brown beneath the
golden glitter of Tinsel Town...where arson, pay-offs, and
porn are all part of the game.

CLANDESTINE   **81141-3/$3.95 US/$4.95 Can**
Nominated for an Edgar Award for Best Original Paperback
Mystery Novel. A compelling thriller about an ambitious
L.A. patrolman caught up in the sex and sleaze of smog city
where murder is the dark side of love.

KILLER ON THE ROAD   **89934-5/$4.50 US/$5.50 Can**
Enter the horrifying world of a killer whose bloody trail of
carnage baffles police from coast to coast and whose only
pleasure is to kill...and kill again.

Featuring Lloyd Hopkins

BLOOD ON THE MOON   **69851-X/$3.95 US/$4.95 Can**
Lloyd Hopkins is an L.A. cop. Hard, driven, brilliant, he's
the man they call in when a murder case looks bad.

BECAUSE THE NIGHT   **70063-8/$3.95 US/$4.95 Can**
Detective Sergeant Lloyd Hopkins had a hunch that there
was a connection between three bloody bodies and one
missing cop...a hunch that would take him to the dark heart
of madness...and beyond.